"I'M LEAVING TODAY, ALEX," NICOLE WARNED. "THIS can't happen."

He gave in to his urge to touch her glorious hair. "What can't happen?"

She blushed—the first real sign she was as aware of him as he was of her. His heart soared crazily.

"This . . ." She lifted her hands helplessly. "This thing between us. It's not right, I've only known you one day."

"And you're leaving," he added for her.

"Yes," she whispered, lifting her gaze to his. "I'm leaving."

Well, then he'd take his chances. Truth was, not much could have stopped him. Slowly, he lowered his head toward hers, watching as her gaze settled on his lips. She licked hers and it took all his self-control to stay steady. When their mouths were a fraction of an inch apart, he murmured, "So this is good-bye, then?"

Her wild eyes locked with his. "Alex—"

"Shhh. I'm only going to kiss you. . . ."

WHAT ARE *LOVESWEPT* ROMANCES?

They are stories of true romance and touching emotion. We believe those two very important ingredients are constants in our highly sensual and very believable stories in the LOVESWEPT *line. Our goal is to give you, the reader, stories of consistently high quality that may sometimes make you laugh, sometimes make you cry, but are always fresh and creative and contain many delightful surprises within their pages.*

Most romance fans read an enormous number of books. Those they truly love, they keep. Others may be traded with friends and soon forgotten. We hope that each LOVESWEPT *romance will be a treasure—a "keeper." We will always try to publish*

LOVE STORIES YOU'LL NEVER FORGET
BY AUTHORS YOU'LL ALWAYS REMEMBER

The Editors

Loveswept® 845

TELL ME NO LIES

JILL SHALVIS

BANTAM BOOKS
NEW YORK · TORONTO · LONDON · SYDNEY · AUCKLAND

TELL ME NO LIES
A Bantam Book / July 1997

ISBN 0-553-44600-2

Published simultaneously in the United States and Canada

Bantam Books are published by Bantam Books, a division of Bantam Doubleday Dell Publishing Group, Inc. Its trademark, consisting of the words "Bantam Books" and the portrayal of a rooster, is Registered in U.S. Patent and Trademark Office and in other countries. Marca Registrada. Bantam Books, 1540 Broadway, New York, New York 10036.

PRINTED IN THE UNITED STATES OF AMERICA

OPM 10 9 8 7 6 5 4 3 2 1

To Michelle,
for being my "real" sister

PROLOGUE

Annoyance shot through Nicole Sanders, and with it came the expected guilt, even though she knew better than to waste her time on either emotion. Especially now.

The casket was covered in roses, set gingerly next to the open grave. Her grandmother had loved roses. It was the only personal thing she knew about the woman.

Mourners surrounded Nicole at the surprisingly lovely grave site. Dark, muted colors, hushed voices, the occasional sniffle . . . all healthy signs the living were grieving a woman who had been well respected and loved by all. She had returned that love freely—to everyone except her son's daughter, Nicole.

The minister stepped up to the head of the site and started speaking in soft, consoling tones that belied the gorgeous spring day around him. Another irritation. Since when, in San Francisco, did it *not* rain in spring?

The minister reminded everyone how loving and generous Maddie Sanders had been, and it was all Nicole could do to not give a very unladylike snort of disgust.

2

She was alone, had been for her entire twenty-seven years. Never had she been given the permanent, guaranteed love of a sibling or a parent, and much as she wanted to deny it, it was important. She knew nothing about her own parents, and even less about her background. It no longer mattered that her grandmother had resented each and every little thing about her. What did matter was that with her death, Nicole was truly, completely alone.

The murmuring increased and Nicole realized the short service was over. People were threading their way to the casket to drop flowers and quietly share their thoughts. She was surrounded by people who had decorated her grandmother's life, and she didn't know one of them. She turned and made her way toward her car, her heart aching for what might have been.

"Excuse me. Oh, excuse me, please wait!"

Standing next to her car, Nicole watched the tall, modellike blonde perilously make her way on the stone path. It couldn't have been easy in those ridiculously spiked heels and runway-perfect suit, but the woman was determined. She smiled brightly—something Nicole immediately mistrusted. Since there was nowhere to run, she braced herself for unwanted sympathy.

"Whew! What a hike." The flawlessly made-up woman put a well-manicured hand to her chest and smiled again. "Nicole Sanders, right?"

Exhaustion was creeping up on her from two sleepless nights that had nothing to do with her demanding job and everything to do with loneliness. Surprisingly close to tears, Nicole stifled her sigh. Patience was not even an option. "I'm sorry, but I'm very busy now."

"I know." The woman stepped closer. Nicole could smell the expensive perfume, hear the chic jewelry jingle on the woman's wrists. "I'm Susan Wilson." When Nicole just looked at her, she said quickly, "I drove all the way from Sunrise Valley and—"

Nicole turned away and opened her door. "This is really a bad time." She was being rude now, and she hated that. But if she wasn't left alone in the next five seconds, she was going to self-destruct. Work, as always, would be her salvation. The kids, her special kids, would revive her as only they could.

"I just wanted to talk to you about your family."

Nicole's insides lurched painfully as she let her hands drop. *Family.* She had none. Her parents had been killed in a car accident when she was one week old. Now her father's mother, her only remaining relative, was gone as well. "I have no family."

The woman's face softened, highlighting her beauty. "You really don't know who I am, do you?" She laughed then, looking absolutely delighted with herself. "I'm the daughter of your mother's brother. Your first cousin. *Family.*"

"You must be mistaken." Heart pounding, Nicole shoved sweaty palms into her pockets. "My mother is dead, and she had no living family."

Susan cocked her lovely head. "But of course she does." Fishing in her purse, she dragged out a picture . . . a wedding picture. Nicole recognized her mother in a pretty white lace dress, her father standing next to her in a suit. His mother stood there, too, wearing a frown of disapproval.

"That man, there on the other side of your mother. That's her brother, Ted. My father."

Torn between the need to believe and the automatic urge to protect herself from disappointment, Nicole didn't know what to say. If it was a joke, it was an exceptionally cruel one. Because for her entire life, the only thing she'd wanted more than love and acceptance was family. "Why now?" she demanded. "After all this time?"

Again, that warm smile. "We just found you. Won't you come to Sunrise Valley? Come visit us, Nicole. Come get to know us."

"But why—"

"Please, Nicole. I'll—we'll—answer all of your questions, I promise."

Answers. All her life she'd waited. Joke or not, she'd go. She couldn't have stayed away.

ONE

Alex Coleman propped a booted foot on the rock he considered his alone, and stared into the shimmering water of Sunrise Valley Lake. As a small boy, this spot had been his salvation from prying, noisy sisters. As a teenager, it had been his make-out spot. Now, as a grown man, the small, private clearing relaxed him as no other place could. Spring in the lush High Sierras was sweet indeed. Surrounded by tall, full pines, white-capped mountain peaks, and clear, crisp air, it seemed wrong to feel discontented and out of sorts.

Dark, threatening clouds moved in from the west. It would rain soon. He should get back before it began. A small rock caught his attention, and he leaned low, skimming it across the lake, pleased when it jumped four times. The next one jumped five. Another personal record—and one that meant nothing.

He needed a challenge, a purpose. He knew running a major ski resort and managing the surrounding land and its properties should have been enough. It wasn't.

At the sudden flash of lightning, he glanced up. A

woman was making her way down the steep path, struggling a little bit, flinching at the sharp crack of thunder. Definitely not a local. No local would attempt the steep path in a bright yellow sundress and sandals.

After another jag of lightning, then the deafening roar of thunder, large drops began to pelt the ground. Stepping off his rock and onto the path, Alex spared the woman another glance and his gaze collided with the most expressive amber eyes he'd ever seen. Fear, confusion, and annoyance swirled in their depths, and despite the downpour, he stopped on the path in front of her. Immediately she turned, moving back up the path, pushing at her dripping auburn hair. Her obvious irritation at the weather amused him, but that she appeared afraid of him did not.

Alex stepped back and slipped his hands in his pockets. "Careful," he called quietly. "It's slippery." When she stumbled slightly, he moved without thinking and grabbed her arm.

Ripping free, she backed up, eyes wide. Her breathing hitched. "I'm fine," she said, blinking furiously as the rain continued to drench them both. Scrambling, she started up the path again.

The smart thing was to just let her go, but there was something about her that drew him. He'd always been a sucker for a damsel in distress. Waiting until she nearly fell again, he caught up with her in two steps. More gently this time, he took her bare arm, thinking she felt so slight and vulnerable. And cold. "Here," he said in what he hoped was a nonthreatening voice. "At least let me help you up this hill. You're going to kill yourself in those sandals."

She stiffened. "I can do it." With a last wrench of her

arm, she raised her lovely chin and turned again. Then promptly fell to her knees in the mud.

Nicole spared one brief second to close her eyes in mortification before struggling to her feet. Rain came down in buckets around her, and she cursed her stupidity. Because of a whimsical wish to see the gorgeous lake up close, she was now alone in the woods with a man she didn't know. Her car sat several hundred yards out of sight.

Why hadn't she gone directly to Susan's place? Her directions, tossed on the front seat, were clear enough. *Nerves, plain and simple.* About to meet the family she'd only fantasized about was wreaking havoc with her insides.

"Here." The man reached a hand out slowly, his face open and friendly. Eyeing him warily, she took it long enough to stand, then flinched at the next crack of thunder. Storms terrified her, had since she'd been a child, though she hated to be afraid of anything.

"Just thunder," he said mildly. "I didn't mean to startle you." His voice was as strong and sure as his hands had been on her a moment earlier. "Are you all right?"

The guy was too tall and broad for her comfort, and in the dim light of the storm she imagined all sorts of terrible things he could do to her there in the privacy of the woods. "I'm fine." She risked a glance over her shoulder. Too far to make a break for it. "Thank you."

He nodded, his gaze briefly running down the length of her. "Do you have far to go? You're soaked."

The wary city girl in her wondered why he wanted to know. "My car is just up the path." Keeping her face perfectly straight, she added, "And my boyfriend's waiting in it."

His mouth twitched, but he nodded solemnly. "Okay."

She started up the path again, and he took her arm in a grip made of iron. "What are you doing?" she asked in a panic, trying unsuccessfully to pull away.

"Just making sure you get back to your boyfriend in one piece." He glanced at her, his lips curved. "Unless, of course, you'd rather swim."

"Funny."

"The roads will be slippery. Do you have far to drive?"

She met his affable, curious gaze. His gray eyes matched the rain-filled skies. "I'm not certain."

"Are you lost?" he asked, the water dripping down his face distorting his expression.

"No, I'm not lost." Why did most men assume that a woman alone was lost? "Besides, my boyfriend's in the car."

"Right."

There was no hiding his amusement this time, and she gritted her teeth. The man didn't even have the courtesy to be out of breath. The ease with which his long, powerful legs churned up the path told her he'd been there thousands of times before.

It was cold. A glance down told her how transparent her wet sundress had become—and exactly how cold she was. She wished for a sweater. Make that a jacket.

"Here," he said, stopping. Releasing her arm, he yanked down the zipper of his hooded windbreaker and pulled it off. "It's wet, but warm."

Nicole just stared at him in dismay, wondering if he could really read her mind. With an exasperated sound, the man pulled it around her shoulders, waiting until she thrust her arms into the sleeves before he bent over her to zip it. He was right, it was warm, incredibly so, with a faint scent of woodsy soap, wet skin, and something else she almost didn't recognize—pure male. She allowed herself one heavenly sniff before resuming her mistrust. Would an attacker, no matter how ridiculously handsome, offer her his jacket?

He pulled her around the last bend of the path and into the dirt pull-off where she'd parked. "*This* is your car?"

She looked at him, raising her chin slightly. Next to the Blazer, which she assumed was his, sat her prized possession, a 1974 VW Bug. She'd had it since she'd been eighteen. It was the only piece to her past she owned. "What's wrong with it?"

"It's a *Volkswagen.*"

"So?"

With a look that obviously questioned her sanity, he spoke slowly. "You can't drive these roads in a storm with a car like that." He pointed to his Blazer. "You need something like mine." As if to emphasize his point, lightning lit the sky and thunder rolled.

The dirt lot she'd parked in not fifteen minutes earlier looked like an extension of the lake. Her tires sat partially covered in mud, probably useless.

"Where's the boyfriend?" he asked, sounding as if he suddenly really wished one would materialize.

She closed her eyes and didn't answer. The rain continued to coat them as they stood in silence.

"How far are you going?" the man asked finally, sighing.

At least he wasn't laughing at her, but she caught the

impatience in his voice. "I'm not exactly sure," she murmured.

"Great." He paused. "Look, I'll give you a lift into town. You could call someone."

Miserably, she stared at the poor car, thinking just five days before there would have been no one to call.

"Look, I can't just leave you out here." He shielded his eyes from the rain and nodded to her car. "That's not going anywhere anytime soon."

That was true, she thought dismally. "All right. I'm going to the Wilson House." The name rolled off her tongue easily enough, and it should. She'd thought of little else for five long days and nights now. It was the bed-and-breakfast inn Susan and her brother, Brad, owned. Nicole had agreed to come for the weekend, if only to prove that she'd not been fooled by Susan's claim.

Alex just stared at her. "You're kidding."

"Never mind," she said, shaking her head and stepping in the mud toward her car. She would simply wait out the storm. Anything would be better than hitching a ride with a stranger whose eyes seemed to see too much.

"I know where it is," he said finally. "I'll take you."

She didn't know whether to be relieved or sorry. The rain came down in torrents, running in tiny rivers down the lean features of his face, making it impossible to read his expression. No matter how wet and stuck she was, her instinctive lack of trust made her hesitate. It didn't help that he looked like a man who was very used to getting his way. With a black shirt tucked into black jeans with black boots, he was missing only the black jacket, which she now wore. For all she knew, he could kidnap her, take her anywhere, do anything—

"Are you going to get in?" He held the door for her,

eyes laughing. "Or maybe you want to wait for that boy-friend of yours?"

Great, a smart-ass.

"Because we could stand out in this weather and chat some more, if you want."

Would a potential bad guy waste time on sarcastic remarks? Or a charming smile meant to disarm? Some of her panic must have shown on her face because his expression softened as the rain slid over them. "We sort of missed the formalities, didn't we?" He smiled then, a self-deprecating smile that lit up his features. "I'm Alex Coleman, owner of the Wilson House."

One shock after another, her muddled brain thought. *Owner.* Susan had told her she ran the place with her brother. Oh no, this man couldn't be . . . related to her? The coincidence defied description. The strange regret didn't bear explanation.

"Hurry. You'll freeze out here," he urged, pushing her gently into the Blazer.

She made the decision to go with him as simply as that. She had her small purse on a long strap across her shoulder. Her overnight bag and car could wait until later. Alex came around and folded his long legs into the Blazer. As he eased out of the lot he turned up the heater and glanced at her. "It will warm up in a second." His gaze shot to the skirt of her dress, which dripped all over the floor, and he shook his head.

Setting her jaw defiantly worked as a bonus. It helped stop the teeth from chattering right out of her head. "It didn't look like rain a little while ago."

"That's true, uh . . ." He looked at her with a question. "This is where you tell me your name."

If he was part of her family, certainly she'd get a

reaction to her name. "Nicole," she said, studying him carefully. "Nicole Sanders."

"Nicole," he repeated softly with a slight smile. His eyes met hers. "It suits you."

God, the man had a pair of eyes. And a manner that even the most unresponsive of women would have a hard time resisting. It was a good thing she was *especially* unresponsive. The windshield wipers squeaked noisily back and forth in rhythm with the driving rain that pelted the window. The car suddenly seemed too small and . . . warm.

"Great weather," she muttered.

He laughed, a light, carefree laugh that Nicole knew to most people would be contagious. Not to her, though she envied it. Laughter didn't come easily to her, neither did interacting with others, but suddenly she felt some of her resistance fall away. Shocked at herself, she turned to him, saw that he smiled at her, and she felt a fluttering low in her belly. Nerves, she told herself. Pure nerves.

"Have you ever been here before?" He turned off the highway onto Sunrise Valley's main street.

"No." She couldn't keep her eyes off the town from the second it came into view. A tiny alpine town, it consisted of no more than a few streets surrounded by a little residential section, but she loved it instantly.

"Are you staying long?"

"No." She had only the weekend, had to be back teaching by Monday.

"The slopes are closed now, not enough snow," Alex said conversationally. "What brings you up here?"

The need for the truth. "Oh, lots of things," she said evasively. Her stomach rattled as they got closer. Large banners advertising an upcoming summerfest hung across the street. Arts, crafts, food . . . it sounded so lovely.

A gust of wind pushed at the Blazer. "Where're you from?"

She turned a purposely cool eye on him, as always, uncomfortable talking about herself. "Playing cab-driver?"

He shrugged, uninsulted, and again gave her that easy smile that almost had her smiling back. "I'm curious. Let me guess. . . ." His gaze ran down the length of her, and her amusement backed up in her throat. "Big-city girl, definitely," he said, "San Francisco?"

"Do you always ask so many questions of your customers?"

"Bad habit," he agreed, without looking apologetic in the least. "But I did save you a long walk."

White knight or not, she had no intention of telling him a thing. They passed the turn for Sunrise Valley Resort and Nicole knew from Susan's map they were almost to the Wilson House. Her stomach tightened again and she bit her lip.

"You okay?"

"Fine." But she wasn't. No matter how she tried, she couldn't relax. God, she was so nervous. She needed to confront Susan, demand answers for all her questions. But she hated confrontations and rarely handled them well.

"You don't look fine." Alex's voice was gruff with concern. "You're white as a sheet." Reaching out, he touched her hand that gripped her stomach and made a sound of concern. "And you're trembling."

They came to a stop sign. With no other cars in sight, Alex apparently felt comfortable remaining in the intersection. "What's the matter?" His eyes narrowed thoughtfully. "Are you running from something? Someone?"

The rough timbre his voice had taken on told her he was more than perfectly willing to go to battle for a woman he hardly knew. Never in her entire life had anyone wanted to protect her, and as ridiculously sexist as it was, it touched her deeply.

The rain beat steadily against the top of the Blazer, and the heater blasted warm air on her legs. It was soothing, as was his voice, and it lulled her into speaking of the bizarre happenings that had led her there. "Not running from," she admitted. "But to."

His gaze held hers, his warm, firm hand still on her arm. "I don't understand."

"I learned last week I had living relatives I didn't know about." He looked relieved, and Nicole imagined it was because he wouldn't have to fight a dragon to save her from evil.

"How did that happen?"

Nicole, after being badgered for the last five days by Susan, had finally agreed to come meet Susan's brother, their father, Ted, and his sister, Candy. A total of two cousins, an uncle, and an aunt. The questions continued to bombard her brain. Susan had promised to answer everything—if Nicole came.

But *why* was there family? *Why* hadn't she been told? *Why* had they waited so many years to contact her? She so desperately needed to know.

"It's a long story," she told Alex now as a car came up behind them. His wide shoulders shifted beneath his wet shirt in interesting ways as he thrust them back in gear. Nicole dragged her gaze away, appalled that she'd noticed such a thing. "I'm going to meet them today."

"And you're nervous."

"Very." She nodded grimly. And foolish enough to make herself look a complete mess, she thought, patting at her hair.

"I'm sure how you look won't matter a bit," he assured her generously, those eyes sparkling.

She stared at him suspiciously, then reached up above her to pull down the visor and peer in the mirror. Moaning, she closed her eyes and sat back. Mascara ran down her face, mud smeared one cheek, and her shoulder-length hair was plastered to her head.

"You could have told me how I looked."

Pulling into the parking lot, he glanced at her innocently. "Okay. You look great."

"*Great*," she repeated with a little laugh. "It's a scary thing, having you drive when you're so obviously blind as a bat. Susan said casual," she muttered, swiping at the mud on her face with the napkin he offered her. "But I doubt she meant it so literally."

Beside her, he went unnaturally still. "*Susan?*"

"Apparently we're first cousins."

"Cousins?" he repeated in a strange voice. "But Candy doesn't have kids."

"No," she said softly. "But her sister, Ella, did."

Pinching the bridge of his nose with his thumb and forefinger, he closed his eyes. Then turned off the engine, moving to face her. His slate eyes showed none of his earlier warmth.

He was angry, she realized. *She*, however, was confused as hell. "*You* own the inn?"

"Yes," he said tersely, completely withdrawn. "Susan and Brad work for me."

Had Susan deliberately misled her, or had Nicole misunderstood?

"Tell me," he said in a very quiet voice. "How did you go all this time without knowing about them?"

She had no idea what made her tell him. Maybe it was his compelling eyes, or his strained voice that told her how much he needed to know. Maybe it was because he'd saved her today, taken time out of his day for her—something she wasn't used to. "My paternal grandmother told me I had no other relatives. I believed her until last week."

Alex sat facing her, the inn and the pounding, relentless rain long forgotten. One long arm draped behind her on the back of the seat, the other on his lean thigh. She felt surrounded by him, and much to her surprise, it wasn't an unpleasant experience.

"What happened last week?" Alex asked finally.

"Susan came to my grandmother's funeral," she said a little breathlessly, wondering why his nearness affected her breathing.

Some of his toughness drained. "I see."

She knew he didn't *see* at all. After her parents' death, she'd grown up in a series of foster homes, shifting frequently at the whim of the system, because her grandmother hadn't wanted her. "Susan read her obituary and came to the funeral hoping to meet me."

The disbelief was back. "Why now? Why not years ago?"

She offered Susan's excuse. "They didn't know where to find me."

His eyes narrowed. "That seems difficult to believe."

Just because she wanted a family so very badly didn't mean she'd lost her common sense. She wondered too. But she'd had to come, as much as she had to take her next breath.

"Well, either you really believe Susan's story," he said, a sardonic half smile twisting his lips, "or she's even quicker than I gave her credit for."

"I don't understand."

"Don't you?" He eyed her intently. "I wonder."

TWO

Watching from the steps of the Wilson House as Alex drove off, Nicole pulled his jacket closer around her and suppressed a shiver. He hadn't acted strange until he'd found out who she was. *Why?*

Her pulse leaped as she took her first good look at the Victorian-style farmhouse, with its three stories and wraparound veranda. Smoke rose from two chimneys, disappearing high among the surrounding trees.

As she stepped inside, the enticing scent of freshly baked bread beckoned her. The entranceway opened up into a large living room, where a loud crackling sound drew her eyes to a brick fireplace.

Nicole fell in love.

Susan appeared out of nowhere with a smile and a warm hug. "You came." She pulled back with a gasp. "Oh! You're drenched!"

Nicole wiggled uncomfortably at the casual affection, then allowed herself to be seated in the large room in front of the fire. "I don't mean to sound rude," she said immediately, "but I'd really like to know how you're so certain we're truly related."

"Not one for small talk, are you?" Serenely, as if she entertained long-lost family every day, Susan poured tea. "I have pictures I'm sure you'd be interested in. And, yes, we're definitely related—you have only to look in the mirror to know that."

Pictures. Nicole sagged back against the sofa, her limbs like Jell-O. To be offered something of her past . . . it nearly brought tears to her eyes. "You seemed surprised to see me just now."

Carefully, Susan stirred her tea. "Well, there was that silly family feud. Brad and I weren't sure how you'd feel about seeing us."

"Feud?" Nicole asked weakly. A vise gripped her heart. "You've always known about me?"

Susan's bright smile faded slightly, and she put down the fragile china. "Of course." She faltered at Nicole's expression. "You knew about us. . . ."

Nicole shook her head, struggling to think past the blinding ache behind her eyes. "No, I didn't know about any of you." The front door opened behind them, but Nicole didn't even notice as she stood abruptly. They'd left her alone all those years.

Susan looked distressed. "Nicole—"

"You didn't need that obituary to find me, did you?" Susan's eyes spoke the truth. "You knew where I was all along. You've always known. Why would you lie?"

"I didn't," Susan denied. "I didn't know *exactly* where you lived. Please, Nicole, sit down."

She couldn't, her legs had locked together. "I'm in the phone book." Confusion, and more hurt than she thought possible, flowed through her. "So why now—after all this time?"

"I'm doing this all wrong. Let me get Brad—"

"Nicole asked a valid question, Susan," Alex interjected from where he leaned against the front door, eavesdropping unabashedly. "Why don't you answer it?" He moved closer, his voice low and soft. "Tell her why you lied to get her here. I'm sure we'd both be interested in that one."

"Go away, Alex," Susan said rudely, abandoning all semblance of elegance. "This has nothing to do with you."

Alex tossed a bag to the ground at Nicole's feet. "I went back for this. Figured you'd need it."

Her overnight bag. "Thanks." She stared at it, trying to get her bearings in a world gone mad.

"*You've met?*" Susan asked, looking shocked. "How?"

"Who's met?" A young man in his early twenties slid down the banister, leaping agilely to his feet at the bottom of the stairs. With his sun-streaked blond hair and dashing good looks, he could have been Susan's twin. Eyeing Alex warily, he smiled politely at Nicole.

"Brad!" Susan laughed nervously and quickly introduced Nicole.

"Oh good." Brad grinned good-naturedly. "I thought you were another customer—I didn't want to make another bed."

"Great attitude." This from Alex, who had attitude written all over him.

Betrayal overcame Nicole. Her unanswered questions choked her. She picked up her bag, surprised at how heavily it weighed at her shoulder. It slipped off with a loud thump.

Alex glanced sharply at her, took one look at her face, and picked up her bag. Taking her hand, he pulled her toward the stairs, and Nicole was just upset enough to let him.

"*Where are you going?*" Susan demanded.

On the second-floor landing, Alex hesitated. "They probably were going to give you room five or six. They each have their own bathroom." Turning right, he led her down a hall decorated with bright and cheerful wallpaper that made Nicole grit her teeth.

Alex opened up room six and nodded. "This is it." Tossing her bag on the bed, he moved closer, so that she had to tilt her head back to see his face. Before, at the lake and in the car, she'd been too nervous to really look at him, but she did so now. His dark hair had started to dry, curling against the top of his collar, and that square jaw was tight, his eyes intense. She'd already noticed his shoulders, set wide on the body of an athlete; tall, lean, and incredibly masculine.

Quite simply, he was the most attractive man she'd ever met. And the most distracting. To gain some distance, she moved to the window.

"Are you going to leave?" he asked quietly.

Far below, the brilliant blue of the lake called to her, and her eyes squeezed shut. She could have loved this place. "Tell me why my being related to Susan bothered you."

"That's . . . complicated."

"That bad, huh?"

Low and soft, his laugh emerged as part humor, part frustration. "Yeah."

"They didn't tell me about you, you know. Susan let me think this place was theirs." Turning, Nicole gave him a direct stare. "Why would she do that?"

"That's complicated too." His gaze never left her face. "Does it matter?"

It shouldn't have. What her cousins thought of Alex Coleman wasn't important. What *she* thought of Alex wasn't important. Why she was there and what she was going to do now was. Habit had her wanting to run, dig her head deep into the sand. But the fantasy of having family still lived inside her.

With an easy, nonthreatening gesture, Alex reached out, brushing a wet tendril of hair off her cheek. His fingers lingered, and her stomach tightened. "There's a family resemblance," he said.

Nicole didn't see it—and didn't appreciate being compared with a couple of people she didn't think she liked very much. Or maybe she didn't like the way her skin tingled at his soft touch.

"I'm kidding." He chuckled at her expression. "You might like Candy." His smile gentled, went soft with an understanding that had her swallowing hard. "Why don't you get out of those wet clothes and relax a bit before making any decisions?" he suggested lightly.

Candy would be her aunt. It still seemed so strange—and so desperately appealing.

"I'll be downstairs for a little while. Let me know if you want a ride back to your car."

"Thanks," she murmured. The door shut softly, and she let her body sag against the ledge. Logically, she knew she couldn't blame Susan and Brad for what had happened to her so long ago. Since they were her age, they would have had no control over her fate. But Candy and Ted . . . didn't she at least owe it to herself to find out why they hadn't wanted her? Why, when her parents had died, they'd let her drift from one foster home to another—never even checking on her? Had they assumed her grandmother had taken her in?

From far below, she could hear the drone of voices,

the sounds of other people living their normal lives, and she wondered if hers would ever be normal again.

Alex took the inn steps two at a time. Halfway down, he met Susan and Brad on their way up.

"What's going on?" Susan's eyes held fire, and he knew what that meant. A fight.

In a purposely annoying move, Alex continued down, into their downstairs office. Leaning back against the window ledge, he watched the afternoon sun play against the rain-drenched trees. He loved this mountain, had forever. He'd inherited most of it, including the land the resort and the inn lay on. Of course, back then it'd been nothing but trees and a decaying old house. Only now, years of hard work later, was the resort beginning to thrive.

Things would have been perfect—except for his mother, and her heart of gold. Out of love for her best friend, Catherine, Susan and Brad's mother, his mother had sold the bed-and-breakfast business she'd made so successful, while retaining for Alex the land and the inn itself. Things had been fine, until Catherine had died—leaving Susan in charge. In the two years since, there'd been nothing but trouble. Now Alex was stuck with the sorry choice of hurting his mother and taking back the business, or letting Susan continue to drain him of cash.

"What are you up to this time, Susan?" he asked wearily.

"I should be asking you."

He glared at her, and she shrugged. "Just getting to know my cousin."

Alex unwittingly conjured up the exotic vision Nicole had made standing on the path, with the stormy lake as a backdrop to her very wet, sheer dress, water dripping enticingly off every curve. A hot stab of arousal bolted through him as he thought how they'd sat in his Blazer, lost in their own world; the warm heater chugging, their clothes steaming, the windows fogged, the rhythmic beating of the rain their only music.

Then he'd discovered who she was, and he'd wanted only to get as far away as possible. Now he realized she was just an innocent pawn in another of Susan's games. Having been at the receiving end of enough of those games himself, he knew Nicole would get hurt.

For years Alex had felt honest sympathy for Susan and Brad. Their father never had time for them, they'd lost their mother, and now had only each other. But it was hard to remain compassionate when they were running his property into the ground.

"Today is your deadline," he told them.

Brad remained typically silent, letting Susan run the show.

"We need more time," Susan said evenly, inspecting her glossy red nails. "I told you that."

Her confidence irked him, as did her composure, especially since he'd been nothing but patient with them both, and he was the only one with anything to lose. "Look," Alex said, struggling with his own temper. "Out of respect for what my mother felt for your mother, I gave you money to jump-start the inn, and you were to buy me out within two years. But not only can't you do that—you need more!" He looked at each of them, knowing he wouldn't get through unless he played the bad guy. "So here's the new deal. I'm here to stay."

"No!" Susan exclaimed, straightening, and showing her first real emotion. "It's *my* business. My mother gave it to *me*."

Alex softened his voice, unable to speak cruelly, even now when he smelled a trap. A trap that had Nicole's name on it. "I've put in too much to back out now."

"Oh, go home," she said unkindly. "Go drool over your expansion plans for the resort—the ones the locals will never approve. I'll get you the lease money I owe you."

He froze. "What do you know of my plans for expansion?"

Susan merely smiled and shrugged.

Not being able to trust his own partners was no way to do business, but he'd been left with no choice. "You'd better hope your cousin doesn't get word of your antics, Susan. If she does, she won't believe a word you say."

"Stay away from her, she's too good for you."

Alex turned toward the door in disgust, and stopped in his tracks.

Nicole stood in the doorway, looking so shell-shocked and confused, his heart ached for her. She'd changed into jeans and a cropped pink sweater.

"What's going on?"

She appeared leery and suspicious—and braced, ready for battle. Not at all what he would have thought someone just meeting her family would look like.

"Nicole, please . . . come in." Susan dropped her hostility faster than Alex could blink.

Brad, wearing a sweet smile, moved forward to hold her hand. "I'm glad you're here, Nicole. It's nice to have more family around."

Under different circumstances, Nicole might have returned his smile, but she pulled her hand free. To make the situation all the more unbearable, she was painfully aware of the tall, rangy man studying them so intently. And who wouldn't be, she thought, glancing quickly at Alex's compelling face, his dark, form-fitting clothes, the ease in which he stood there. His very presence dominated the room, but she forced her gaze to her cousins.

Nicole had spent a good many years being at the end of someone else's rope. Going from place to place on a whim of the system. But no more. Being completely in charge of her own life now was not only a luxury, but a necessity for her sanity. "Obviously, Susan, we had a misunderstanding. You've asked me here for a specific reason." She let out her breath. "I'd like to know what that is."

"I know. And you're brimming with questions, I can see it." Susan sent Alex a look. "Let me just walk Alex to the door—"

A bell rang from somewhere within the inn, and Susan and Brad exchanged an uneasy glance. Then the telephone rang, too, and Brad moaned. Susan sighed and stood. "I'm sorry." Alex received a long look. "I'll be *right* back," she said. "Brad, phone?"

Alex waited until both Susan and Brad had moved reluctantly from the room before he said casually, "I knew your mother."

"You did?"

"I grew up here. I was only five when she left, but I remember." He looked outside, then back to Nicole. "From now until dinner, your cousins will be swamped. Come outside with me and I'll tell you what I remember."

The useless fury remained, but so did her need for answers.

Opening the office door for her, Alex put a hand lightly on the small of her back as she passed through. It was only a casual gesture, one that a thousand different men might make, but Nicole jumped anyway. Long after his hand had moved, she could still feel the warmth on her skin. It startled her, that a perfect stranger could so unbalance her.

"Ella Anne Wilson loved this place," Alex told her as they stepped from the living room onto the veranda.

Nicole stopped in her tracks, and Alex, who had already stepped off the porch and onto the dirt path below, looked at her in surprise.

"Ella Anne Wilson," she repeated softly, reverently. "I never knew her middle name. Until I met Susan, I didn't even know her maiden name."

He pulled her gently down the steps, keeping his eyes on hers. "Now, that's the loveliest thing I've seen all day."

"What?" she asked, puzzled.

"Your smile."

Her stomach betrayed her by doing a slow roll. Embarrassed, she looked away, but followed him on the narrow path that led through the woods to a small, private beach. The ground squished pleasantly beneath their feet from the recent rain. After the last tension-filled hour, the cool air seemed wonderfully refreshing.

Alex had no idea why he felt so drawn to the woman walking next to him, but he found it difficult to keep his eyes off her. Her worn jeans, soft-looking sweater, and tennis shoes suited her small, subtly curved body perfectly. Her shoulders were impossibly straight, her chin up . . . as if she faced the world alone. He knew he should stay as far away from her as possible, knew the kind of trouble Susan could make for him if he pursued this . . . but he couldn't seem to help himself.

The water lapped gently against the pebbled shore.

More as a habit than anything else, he stooped, picked a rock, and skimmed it across the lake's surface.

Nicole watched, then bent to the ground, making him smile at how meticulously she hunted until she found a rock that pleased her. When she straightened and sent it hurtling across the lake, it bounced five times.

"Not bad for a city girl," he said, impressed.

"I may have been a city girl, but I had a lot of time—" She faltered and fell quiet.

He threw another rock, giving her a minute. She seemed so uneasy around him, and he wanted to know if it was him—or all men. He also sensed a deep-rooted restlessness, something he recognized all too well since he felt it too. "You grew up with your grandmother?"

"No." She bent for another rock, effectively avoiding eye contact. She was good at that, too, he noticed.

When she caught his surprised look at how well she chucked another rock, she shrugged. "I'm a teacher . . . for the mentally challenged. We spend a lot of time doing stuff like this, it's good for them and their self-esteem."

He could picture her with those kids, could picture her smiling at them, challenging them to do their best, smoothing away their tears. She did not belong there. She'd get hurt. The kindest thing he could do would be to send her away. But her eyes, those needy, eager eyes . . . he couldn't do it.

"I'd like to hear more about my mother," she said, shifting uneasily. He blinked, realizing he'd been staring.

"I'm just trying to figure out how much you already know."

She chucked a rock with a strength that surprised him. "Since I know absolutely nothing, I doubt you'll bore me."

"All right." Maybe, he thought, just maybe she had the inner strength to deal with this. He hoped. "I never knew your mother's father. He died young. Your mother's mother was what some called overbearing and strict."

Nicole had stopped throwing rocks and stared at him, enraptured, making his heart twist, and he could have cheerfully twisted Susan's neck for not enlightening her properly. It was hard for him to remember Ella, he'd only been a very young boy. But for the woman looking at him so expectantly, he'd try. "I remember Ella as kind, loving, and very carefree. But her mother didn't agree with her choice of a husband. Ella wouldn't budge, and your grandmother threatened to disown her."

"How cruel!" Color draining from her face, she sank to the soft sand. "I'm sorry, I have to sit. To hear something, anything at all, makes me feel shaky."

He sat next to her. "I come from a large family," he told her. "Four sisters. We're close." With satisfaction, he watched as some of the color returned to her cheeks. "I don't pretend to understand how someone could willingly decide to give up her own flesh and blood, but that's what happened. And Ella felt she had no choice but to pick her man over her family. We never saw her again."

A myriad of emotions crossed her face; sympathy for the mother she never knew, anger at the grandmother who had caused the pain in the first place, and a sad regret to find it all in the past, and therefore unchangeable. "It later turned out that she was pregnant with you all along. She'd only been gone six months when she had you."

"And then she was killed in that car wreck." Nicole sat quietly, her eyes on the lake. "I've imagined her.

Over and over again, in a hundred different ways. It's nice to know the truth." Some of her sadness seemed to drain. "She was a woman so dedicated to the baby she carried and the man she loved that she'd been willing to give up her family for them." Her lovely eyes glistened as her gaze met his. "Thank you."

"I wish there was more I could tell you, but that's about all I know of her." Then, because he couldn't resist, he took her hands in his. Her look of surprised pleasure tugged at him, had him running his thumb over her knuckles.

"I should get back," she said a little nervously, pulling her hands away. "I want to meet Ted and Candy before I go."

Disappointment settled over him. "You're leaving today, then?"

"That depends."

He knew without being told, Nicole expected a damn good reason from Susan as to why she'd contacted her now. It was something he was interested in as well, for much as he didn't want to think it, Susan was up to no good. And he would bet it had something to do with him.

"Hope you haven't been bored," Susan said, coming into the living room.

Not likely. "I have plenty to think about," Nicole said.

"Yes, I guess you do." Susan's look was pensive but calm. Every piece of blond hair was perfectly tucked into place, her lips glossed, her suit wrinkle-free. It amazed Nicole because after a day of work she always looked like a wreck.

"I'm sorry, Nicole."

"Don't be, just tell me the truth."

"All right. It's simple, really. I wanted a sister."

It had been Nicole's greatest fantasy. When she was a kid, other girls wished for toys or the latest Barbie. She wished for family. "So why didn't you call me sooner?"

Susan's eyes met hers, then skittered away. "I didn't want to intrude in your life."

"You—" She had to take a deep breath, then stood. "When I think of how many times I just wanted to know I belonged somewhere—" *No.* She wouldn't let herself show how much that hurt. As she would have cautioned her more volatile students, she took a deep breath. It was over and done, those years of shifting from place to place were long gone. She had herself now and managed just fine.

"Grandmother had forbidden my father and Candy to have any contact with your mother after she left. *Forbidden,* Nicole. And she meant business."

Her answer wasn't good enough. "She's dead now, and from what Alex told me, she's been gone for some time."

Susan's lips thinned. "Alex had no right to tell you anything."

"That's right," Nicole agreed. "*You* should have told me."

"We thought Maddie would have told you. We figured you'd come to us if you wanted."

"Maddie told me nothing." Nicole found herself shaking and had to sit back down.

"I didn't know," Susan said slowly, her eyes filled with regret. "I need you, Nicole. If that makes me selfish, well then, I'm guilty."

Miserably, Nicole stared at her. "I want to talk to your father and Candy. Are they coming?"

"They'll be here tomorrow."

Before Nicole could comment on how strange that seemed, Alex strode into the room, his intense eyes immediately seeking her out, and suddenly it was impossible to concentrate on anything but him.

THREE

With Alex's large, strong presence, the room seemed suddenly smaller—certainly full of electric currents, given the silent and hostile look he and Susan exchanged.

From his pocket he pulled the keys Nicole had given to him earlier. "Your car's safe in the lot."

"Thanks." Her stomach did a funny little lurch when his warm hand connected with hers.

"I was just about to ask Nicole to consider coming to stay with us for the summer," Susan said to Alex. "Being a teacher, she'll have the entire three months free."

"I couldn't," Nicole protested. *Wouldn't.* "I always get a summer job." Especially if she wanted to continue eating on a regular basis.

"You could work here," Susan said quickly, glancing at Alex. "Couldn't she? We need the help."

Alex nodded, watching Nicole carefully. "Of course she'd be welcome."

It was as simple as that, Nicole thought. She needed a job, they'd provide one. What were families for? Her gaze met Alex's and she was forcibly reminded by the heat she found there—he was *not* her family. Biting her lip, she backed up, mentally and physically.

"Nicole—" Susan stepped toward her, but Alex stopped her.

"Give her some space, Susan," he said evenly, his gaze still on Nicole. "Stop pushing. For once."

Nicole needed to think, and she couldn't do that with Susan's needy eyes on her, or with Alex's, which seemed to see far more than she would have liked. "I think I'll go upstairs."

Susan jumped up, eager to please. "Let me get you some tea to take to your room."

When she'd gone, Alex smiled at her. "You okay?"

Why did he have to have a smile that most women would die for? All her life she'd managed to avoid any serious entanglements with the male species. Now, when she needed to be able to think clearly, a mere curving of this man's lips left her deaf, blind, and stupid.

"I'm fine."

His gaze roamed her features. "You're not. They're just people," he said quietly. "They can't possibly live up to your expectations."

His voice, so gentle, served only to humiliate her. Of course she knew they were only people, with very human faults. She herself was all too human, as her strange attraction to him proved. "I'm a big girl, Alex. I can take care of myself."

"You're used to that, I imagine." He tucked a strand of her hair behind her ear and smiled.

At just that little connection of his skin to hers, an inner heat stole through her, owing nothing to the warmth of the room. To gain perspective—and distance—she turned away. "Yes, I am."

"It's okay to lean on someone once in a while."

She wouldn't know.

"I know you hardly know me . . . but you could lean on me."

That, she thought, staring up into his handsome face, would be a big mistake. "No. Thank you." To clear her head, she turned away.

"Nicole," he said solemnly. "Just don't expect too much. I don't want to see you hurt." Gently, he turned her back to face him, searching her features. "I've upset you." His eyes were dark and relentlessly intense. "But it's the truth."

"I'm a stranger to you. Why do you care?"

Again, that deep look, the one that made it difficult to swallow. "You know better than that. Already we're no strangers." Then, after a slight hesitation, he headed for the door. "Sleep well, Nicole."

Damn him, she thought, moving after him. "Hurt how?" she asked, unable to let it go. "How could they possibly hurt me more than they already have?"

"I've known them a long time. And I'm afraid that they—that no one—could be what you're expecting."

"What is it you think I'm expecting?"

Lifting a hand to her hair, he fingered a strand. The touch sent a spiraling mix of thrill and confusion through her.

"You're expecting to get a ready-made family, the one you never had," he said softly. "But maybe you should try for something different. Something that has absolutely nothing to do with your family."

She licked her lips nervously. "I . . . don't think so," she whispered. Her life had not been a simple one. Moving more times than she could count, survival had been her first priority in a constantly shifting world.

Trust, friendship, love—things most people took for granted—didn't come easy for her.

"You've learned how to be alone real well, Nicole. Maybe it's time to let someone else in."

"I don't know what you're talking about," she said, lifting her chin. But she was very afraid she did know.

His eyes told her he did, too, as his thumb slid over her chin, evoking a delicious shiver. "You'll figure it out."

She didn't want to dabble in anything so dangerous as flirting, especially with a man so experienced as this one seemed to be. "I don't play games, Alex."

"I'm not playing with you."

"I'm here to meet my family," she said firmly. "I don't have time for anything else." Because his closeness was disturbing her in strange ways, Nicole's voice sounded shakier than she would have liked. "I mean it."

"I heard you," he said lightly. He lifted her hand and pressed his lips to the knuckles. "You're trembling, Nicole."

She had to bite her tongue rather than say something hurtful.

He released her and smiled knowingly. "Good night."

Then, because she couldn't resist, she peeked her head out the door and watched him walk down the hallway, whistling to himself softly. When he'd disappeared from sight, she touched the hand that he'd kissed, smiling in spite of herself.

Hot, tired, and hungry, Alex pounded another nail in place with satisfaction. He stood back to check the results and liked what he saw. Oh, it was just a plain empty room, only half drywalled now. But by next winter it would be Sunrise Valley Resort's new day-care center.

His growling stomach reminded him that though it was only eight o'clock in the morning, he'd been hard at work for hours. Yes, it was only June, and yes, he had plenty of time before the next snow hit, but manual labor served to keep his mind off his problems—like the unusual trouble he'd had getting city approval for his expansion plans.

Or Susan and her money pit called the Wilson House.

Or a certain auburn-haired, amber-eyed beauty he'd just met—the one whose mouth had said she wasn't interested while her eyes stated the opposite. Lord, he must be insane to be daydreaming about a Wilson. Susan would do her best to tear him to shreds if she knew. Not that he cared what she thought. But Nicole . . . What drew him? Her wide, lovely eyes that spelled out her every emotion, or the soft and vulnerable heart she wore on her sleeve for all the world to see?

It didn't matter, she claimed to have no wish for a relationship, no matter how casual. Just as well, casual relationships had never been his thing. Casual *anything* wasn't his thing. As his family tended to remind him, he was single-minded, in business especially. And it was that very trait that made him so successful. Short-term didn't appeal to him. No, he tended to go into things for the long haul—so when it came to women, he might consider himself . . . well, unsuccessful.

"Alex! I've been looking all over for you," Krista wheezed, leaning against the doorway. "I'm too old for this job."

Alex laughed. The fact that his sister was near forty was hard to believe, and she well knew it. As lithe and agile as a woman half her age, Krista could outrun him—and not only was he in great shape, he was nearly ten years her junior.

Straightening to her full height, which rivaled his own, she moved into the room. "You should carry a beeper like more considerate bosses. It'd be a lot easier on your staff."

He laughed again. "The season is over, you *are* my staff." But he took pity on her. "I'll check in more, I promise. Hey, what are you doing here on a Sunday?"

"That's gratitude for you. I came to finish the accounting. You seemed in a hurry to have the journals from the inn."

"I am." Alex moved toward her, sensing her distress. He might not have had lots of personal relationships with women, but he did understand them. A man couldn't grow up with four sisters and not understand women. "What's the matter? Shelly take on another loony case?"

A corner of Krista's mouth quirked. Shelly, the private investigator—and their baby sister—tended to take on cases out of sympathy rather than practicality. "No."

"Lori or Robin have any more psychic incidents?"

The smile broke on Krista's face at the mention of their twin sisters. Their latest claim that they could read each other's mind had amused the entire family for the past month. "If they did, they're keeping it to themselves. And," she added as Alex started to speak again, "Mom and Dad are fine too. I just got a postcard from someplace in the Caribbean. Their world cruise is a big success." She paused. "Alex, John Mitchell is here."

The fire marshal. "I didn't call for an inspection yet."

Krista raised her shoulders and shook her head.

"Terrific." When he started renovating the small resort, there'd been no comments from the locals, except a casual murmur of pleasure over the slight increase of winter tourism it would bring. Yet this year, when Alex had begun to add on to the place, hoping to become competitive with the neighboring Lake Tahoe resorts, he had found himself up against a brick wall. His permits were delayed, inexplicably. His designs disapproved, over and over again. Inspections were unavoidably postponed or occurred unexpectedly.

"Tell John I didn't request an inspection today."

"I did that. Someone isn't thrilled about the changes you've planned, Alex," Krista said softly. "Do you have any idea who it is?"

"No, dammit." He rolled his shoulders, trying to ease his stress. "Tell him I'll be in the office in a few minutes." He scooped up a handful of nails, shoved them into his tool-belt pocket, and was hammering again before Krista could take two steps out.

He heard the impatient voice calling for him through the pounding of his hammer, but it suited him to ignore it, and he didn't bother to slow until he knew John was standing directly behind him.

"Marshal," he straightened. "What can I help you with?"

The man eyed the room without comment. His sharp, dark eyes turned to Alex. "Just driving by."

"On a Sunday?"

"Thought I'd stop in and see the progress." Although John walked through the large room with a calm, nonchalant air, Alex wasn't deceived. The marshal then surveyed the three other rooms, then the bathrooms, bending and reaching at every plug, overhead light, and switch he saw.

"Find anything you missed on your earlier trips?"

The marshal turned back. "Nope. Hoping for a big season this year?"

"That's the idea." Alex leaned against a wall, his hands in his pockets to keep them from reaching for the man's neck.

When the man finally left, Alex climbed a tall ladder in the center of the room to inspect a flickering light, refusing to speculate on what John *et al* would have in store to delay him next.

Suddenly he stiffened, not needing to hear the soft footsteps behind him or to smell her sexy scent to know Nicole had just entered the room. From the moment they'd met the previous day, there'd existed this strange awareness, almost like a current of electricity running between them.

She walked to the foot of the ladder and looked up uncertainly. With a deep breath, he reminded himself that the intense thrill he got from just the sight of her was merely physical. It could be ignored.

"Hello," she said softly, self-conscious. "I've been walking. The path from the back of the inn led me here."

He raised his eyebrows. The day-care center was located next to the lodge, which was a good quarter mile off the path she referred to, which meant she couldn't possibly have found him by accident.

She flushed. "Well, not *here* exactly. But I met your secretary. Krista?"

He backed down the ladder. "She's my sister."

"Yes, well, she told me where to find you." She moved toward the wide windows, staring at the majestic, snowcapped mountains. When she turned back, Alex held his breath. The early sunlight went right through her light blouse, giving him a peek-a-boo hint of a lacy camisole underneath. Hadn't he just told himself he could ignore his physical response to her? Well, the part he was supposed to ignore was hard enough to hammer nails.

"Remind me to thank her," he managed.

"I came about last night."

Tossing his hammer aside, he took a deep breath. "I'm sorry," he said after a minute. "I moved too fast. It was wrong."

"No," she said quickly. "Not that. I meant . . . well, I never properly thanked you for rescuing me at the lake yesterday, and then moving my car."

"Forget it."

But that became difficult to do when she moved closer, reaching out a hand to run unadorned fingers down a drywall seam. "And I'm sorry I was rude to you when you were so kind."

"I said forget it."

"I can't. I, that is, I . . ." She trailed off nervously.

"What is it, Nicole?"

Her hesitation tipped him off. It came to him like a blow. She wanted something—just as Susan always did. Would it be money again, or something new this time? Would he never learn? "All right," he said tersely. "I'll play. I'll even guess—you need something, right?"

In the face of his bad mood, her nervousness disappeared, as if she were used to defending herself. "Never mind."

What the hell was the matter with him? Cursing himself, he caught up with her at the door. They grappled together with the handle until he looked into those annoyed, confused eyes and sighed. "Nicole, wait."

She didn't.

"Wait, dammit," he said, stepping after her. She kept walking. He grabbed her arm, letting go when she whirled on him, her eyes lit with temper.

"I'm sorry," he said quietly. "I lashed out at you."

"It was wrong to come."

"No," he said, shaking his head. "I—would you just wait a minute?" He found himself talking to empty air and had to run after her. "Look, let's both just start this whole thing over, okay?" Relaxing when she slowed, he forced a casual smile. "I'll start." He lifted a hand in greeting. "Nice to see you again."

Her mouth twitched suspiciously at his polite tone. "Hello."

Relief that she hadn't run made him momentarily stupid. So did her almost smile. "Pretty day," he said inanely.

"Hmmm," she agreed. "Nice day—but, Alex, all I wanted was to know why you think Ted and Candy haven't come to meet me."

The sun cast her face in shadow so he couldn't see her expression. It also highlighted what was under her blouse. "I think if Candy knew you were here," he said slowly, his mind addled by the loss of blood, "she'd have come immediately." He shifted closer, and as he expected, she turned to avoid being in tight proximity, wrapping her arms around herself. The defensive, vulnerable position brought him up short.

How could he not be moved by how small and burdened she looked? Or by her confusion? And how the hell did he maintain the distance she so obviously wanted when all he wanted to do was move closer?

"Well," she said, smiling awkwardly. "That's what I thought too." She moved toward the path from which she'd come.

"Nicole—" What could he say? Sorry that she'd been misled by her selfish, manipulating cousin? He knew the feeling. And even knowing she should, he didn't want to see her leave. If they were anything alike, she'd regret it for the rest of her life. "Nicole, don't go. Not like this."

Tossing down his tool belt, he moved after her. "I know you question why Susan brought you here, but you did come. You must have had reasons for doing so."

"I have a lot of questions."

When she started walking again, he moved along with her. "So don't go before you get them answered. Come on, Nicole. You've got more spunk than that. Get what you want."

"Oh, I intend to get my questions answered." Then, as if she realized for the first time that he had followed her, she stopped short. "Where are you going?"

What made such a beautiful woman so defensive? "I'm walking you back."

She crossed her arms. "I don't need you to show me the way."

"I know you don't need me," he said quietly, before giving in to the urge to touch her glorious hair. "I just want to walk you back."

"I'm leaving today, Alex," she warned, but for the first time she didn't resist his touch. "This can't happen."

"What can't happen?"

She blushed—his first real sign that she was as aware of him as he was of her. His heart soared crazily.

"This . . ." She lifted her hands helplessly. "This thing between us. It's not right, I've only known you one day."

"And you're leaving," he added for her.

"Yes," she whispered, lifting her gaze to his. "I'm leaving."

Well, then, he'd take his chances. Truth was, not much could have stopped him. Slowly, he lowered his head toward hers, watching as her gaze settled on his lips. She licked hers, and it took all his self-control to stay steady, to keep his hands in his pockets. When their mouths were a fraction of an inch apart, he murmured, "So this is good-bye, then?"

Nodding, her wild eyes locked with his. "Alex—"

"Shhh. I'm only going to kiss you." As soft as a whisper, he brushed his lips over hers, savoring the sweet taste of her. The last things he saw before he lost his senses were her stunned eyes wide on his. He trailed his lips lightly over one cheek to her ear, delving, dipping, then making his way back, delighting in her soft sigh. By the time their lips touched again, feathery kisses weren't enough, and they came together with a searing desperation that had them both breathless. He felt her tremble with the same need that shook him, and for a minute he could actually feel what it would be like to be with her, deep inside, with her wrapped around him.

Pulling back slightly, he watched her eyes flutter open, saw the pulse beat frantically at her neck. It undid him. He framed her face softly in his shaking hands and leaned in again—until her eyes widened and she stepped back.

In a gesture that charmed him, she touched her lips. "I gotta go now," she whispered. And she ran off down the path.

So she ran from problems rather than face them. It disturbed him, not only because the kiss had left him wanting her more than he could ever remember wanting a woman, but because he knew how easy it would be for her to leave Sunrise Valley and never look back. She could blame it on Susan's treatment of her. She could blame it on Ted and Candy's disinterest. She could blame it on anything—but herself.

He debated with himself right there on the deserted path. He should let her go, it would be safer for her. She wouldn't get hurt. Neither would he. *Let her go.* But he couldn't. And for the life of him, he didn't know why.

So he followed her.

When the Wilson House loomed in front of a winded Nicole, she slowed, walking through the parking lot, trying to catch her breath.

"Nicole, wait."

She stiffened at his voice, then slowly turned, her eyes drawn to the lips of the man who'd just kissed her. "You . . . *kissed* me," she whispered before she could stop herself. "I mean . . . *really* kissed me."

"Yeah." He smiled in a way that should have irritated her. "Did you like it?"

She bit her lip. Of course she'd liked it, but she shrugged casually. "It was just . . . a little kiss."

Tipping back his head, he laughed. "You're good for me, Nicole." He held out his hand. "All right, then, you asked for it. Come here, I'll show you a bigger, better one."

Better? It wasn't possible. "Oh, no," she said, taking a step back, tucking her hands behind her in a gesture she recognized as childish. Did the man have to be so damn gorgeous? "I don't—"

A loud gasp startled her. Stopping, she stared at the woman five feet away, feeling her own shock drain the blood from her face.

"Oh my God," the woman whispered, staring at Nicole. Her hand flew to her chest. "*Oh, my God.*"

Nicole had the same reaction. The woman and Nicole were virtual mirror images of each other, except for the faint lines of age around the woman's eyes and mouth.

"Ella," the woman said softly, tears springing to her eyes.

FOUR

Nicole staggered back, falling against Alex, who steadied her. He murmured something to her, but she couldn't hear past the roaring of her heart.

"Ella," the woman said again.

"No." Nicole shook her head. "I'm Nicole."

The woman smiled through her misty eyes. "I know, I mean you look just like her—just like she looked when I last saw her."

Nicole swallowed hard against the unaccustomed lump in her throat.

"Nicole, this is Candy," Alex said. "And Candy . . ." He reached out to squeeze the woman's arm gently, as if preparing her. "This is Nicole."

They stared at each other. After a minute Candy moved awkwardly forward, giving her a hug. "Nicole." She held on tight. "Oh, Nicole."

Nicole stiffened from habit, unnerved to find herself being held by someone who so closely resembled her.

"How did you come to be here?" Candy asked.

Before she could express dismay that Candy hadn't

known of her arrival, Alex made a sound, then he cursed beneath his breath. "Here come the troops, ladies," he said grimly. "Brace yourselves."

"Aunt Candy!" Susan called from the steps of the inn. "You're here." She waved them closer and smiled warmly. "Come in, everyone, come in."

Nicole allowed herself to be ushered inside, where they all gathered in the library for privacy, only because she was shaking with the need for some answers. Susan, beautifully composed as always, seemed like the poised matriarch of the family, busily taking charge of the seating arrangements and ordering Brad to get the tea.

Candy's earlier joy at seeing Nicole seemed to have faded somewhat, leaving Nicole even more unsettled. At the window, Alex stood staring at the lake.

"What's going on?" a stern-looking man said from the doorway. Older than Candy and considerably more portly, he still retained the Wilson look with his distinguished, handsome features.

"Dad!" Susan cried, standing. She grabbed her father by the hand and led him to Nicole, making the introductions. She smiled proudly. "Isn't this great?"

The man's eyes lighted briefly on Candy, and they exchanged a long, meaningful look that had Nicole squirming in her chair. She felt absolutely mortified and . . . furious. "I can't believe this," she said, standing. She shook her head at Susan as she went to the door. "You really went too far."

"Wait!" Susan cried, grabbing Nicole's arm. "Please, don't go. I just wanted to surprise them, I knew they'd love it." She whirled to her father, who was still staring in shock at Nicole. "Aren't you thrilled, Dad?"

Ted didn't offer a hand or a hug, just peered at Nicole over his glasses. "You look just like—"

"I know," Nicole said, unable to hide her annoyance. *What was wrong with these people?* "I look like Ella."

Ted sighed. "So much time has gone by. I didn't realize until now, seeing you all grown up. What do we owe this surprise to?"

Not, *how incredible it is to see you.* Not, *I've always wondered how you turned out.* "You owe the surprise to Susan." She would not, would absolutely not, lose it in front of these strangers.

"Isn't it exciting?" Susan asked.

Turmoil. Betrayal. Rage. Her stomach ached with them all. Her eyes shifted to Alex at the window. Did she regret the trip? No, she thought, acutely aware of Alex watching her in return. And for a moment she had the strangest sensation. The sounds of the others talking faded and all she could hear was her own accelerated heartbeat. Alex's cool gray eyes warmed and a silent message seemed to pass from him to her. *It isn't over*, he seemed to tell her. *You can dismiss your family, but you can't dismiss me.* And just as suddenly she couldn't remember why she'd wanted to.

"Nicole?" Susan asked, touching her shoulder. "Didn't you hear Dad?"

Nicole jerked her eyes from Alex, felt her face heat. She focused with difficulty. "I'm sorry."

"This must be slightly overwhelming," Ted said with a calm air that Nicole didn't come close to feeling.

Alex's lips curved, as if he'd heard a silent joke.

Candy, looking more than slightly overwhelmed herself, added, "I've thought about what it would be like to meet you."

"Why didn't you?" Nicole asked. "Meet me, I mean." Everyone stared blankly at her, except Alex. His look was anything but blank. "I never lived in any other city than the one my parents died in. My last name never changed from Ella's married one. Why didn't you contact me sooner?"

Silence.

"Some things are more difficult than you can imagine," Ted said.

In the midst of the heavy, awkward tension that followed, Alex came to her. Casually, possessively, he laid a hand on her shoulder. "As difficult as it may be to discuss, Ted, I imagine Nicole has plenty of questions."

"Of course," Ted said, rising to Alex's unspoken challenge. With an unsmiling face, he turned to Nicole. "I do have some things of Ella's. Maybe I could show you sometime."

Alex's interference seemed disturbingly intimate, but Nicole couldn't regret it. Not when it got her what she wanted. "I'd love that."

She felt Alex's gentle squeeze on her shoulder and glanced at him. His almost imperceptible nod and reassuring eyes not only challenged, but decided her.

Taking a deep breath, she asked, "Since I'll be leaving later, how about now?" She was good at rejection, she reminded herself when no one spoke. It shouldn't hurt so. "I may not get another chance," she said softly, willing to beg.

"I'll take her," Alex said, his voice low, tough.

She had never been so aware of a human being in her life. He stood next to and slightly behind her, an absolute tower of strength and support.

Letting people into her life was not a strong point of hers. But Alex had ignored her resistance, giving her his unconditional friendship regardless.

Her heart warmed a little. Until she looked at him. No, she thought a little wildly, friendship hadn't been the right word. Those eyes of his showed his hunger, his need for far more than friendship.

"Thanks, Alex," Candy said quickly, speaking for the first time. "But you're busy. Ted is too. I'll take her." She smiled uncertainly at Nicole. "I want to."

"Alex is a good man."

Nicole's gaze shot to Candy. They sat on Ted's attic floor, an array of boxes set before them. "Oh?"

"Yes. I've known him a long time."

Nicole hadn't, but felt as though she had. There was something about him . . . something about the way he made her feel, and then there was the way he kissed. Her mouth went dry. "No one else seems overly fond of him."

"There's a lot of history there," she said with a faint smile. "But mostly, in Brad and Susan's case, it's hard to be friends with your boss. And Ted . . . well, he's a doctor. A good one, but sometimes he has a hard time talking to us mere mortals." She smiled fondly, thinking of her brother. "But he's a good man, too, Nicole. Really, he is. He has no problem with Alex." She leaned over and picked up a picture.

While Nicole couldn't wait to dig into the boxes, she couldn't resist asking: "What I'm more interested in, Candy, is what's *your* problem with me?"

Candy dropped the picture she held and stared at Nicole in dismay. "Oh, Nicole. I don't have a problem with you."

But Nicole knelt beside her aunt, her gaze glued to the picture Candy had dropped, riveted by the small piece of history she saw. Three kids rode on a small two-wheeler. They all beamed broadly for the picture—and they all looked alike.

"That's Ella," Candy told her. "And me and Ted." Her smile was soft, nostalgic.

Watching Candy look at the picture, seeing the remembered joy on her face, sent a sharp feeling of envy shooting through Nicole. She had no pictures of her past, no joyful memories.

"I fell off a few minutes after this shot was taken and broke my collarbone." Her smile turned rueful. "Ella was grounded for a month. My mother wasn't too tolerant of that sort of thing. She liked things neat and tidy—which we seldom were."

"Kids shouldn't have to be neat and tidy," Nicole murmured. As a child, Nicole had been the proverbial clean one, a habit born out of self-defense. You couldn't dislike a spotless kid, she'd thought—wrongly. Plenty of times people hadn't liked her or wanted her—and being clean hadn't had a thing to do with it. Knowing Candy, Ted, and her mother shared this with her gave Nicole and Candy unexpected common ground, and a flicker of hope came to life inside her.

"Would you believe me if I told you I've thought about you every single day since the day you were born?" Candy asked her softly.

Nicole sighed and lifted her head. "I don't know."

"I was very young when Ella died, just a teenager. We were best friends, and yet, I wasn't allowed to go to her funeral. I couldn't have taken you then, as much as I wanted to."

"I understand that," Nicole said. "But what about later? All those years went by." She swallowed her pride in exchange for knowledge. She had to have it. "I was so alone. I needed you."

Candy glanced away, as if she couldn't stand the pain and retribution in Nicole's eyes. "I tried to find you when I graduated college. No one at the city or the state level would help me."

How she wanted to believe that. "Susan found me easily enough."

Candy pulled a heavy box toward her. "And I'll be eternally grateful. All this stuff was Ella's. Take whatever you'd like. Make yourself a pile."

From the rooftop deck of the ski lodge, Alex took in the panoramic view. As always, the mountains, bordered by the lush valley and sparkling lake below, soothed him. The road to town cut lazily through his vision, and if he followed it with his eyes, he could just make out the Wilson House and its smoking chimneys.

"It's so beautiful." Krista sighed, coming up beside him. She offered him a soft drink and leaned back against the railing.

He forced his mind off the inn, and the people in it. Especially one Nicole Sanders. "I know. Even after all these years I never get tired of standing here and looking around." He took a long sip.

"You've been working too hard, Alex," she chided gently, reaching for his hand. "I know how much this place means to you, and I know exactly how much work you've put into it, but you should relax a little."

Alex's eyes sharpened on the lone VW he could see moving away from the inn. He couldn't see her, of course, but he knew that Nicole was leaving. The small vehicle chugged down the main road, away from the inn, away from the resort. And out of his life. He wanted to think it didn't matter, that he'd hardly known her.

But it did matter. They'd shared something—a connection—no matter how much Nicole wanted to deny it. He felt her loss keenly, in a way he hadn't thought possible.

"I heard there's a new Wilson in town," Krista said casually, her eyes narrowed on him.

"No," he said, watching the car disappear, feeling a sense of sorrow he'd never experienced. "She's gone."

At home in San Francisco, Nicole kicked off her shoes, plopped down on the couch. She didn't bother to check her mail or phone machine. Her mail would only be junk and her machine pathetically clear of messages. She opened her bag and smiled at the sight of Ella's papers and pictures mixed in with her own clothes. It made it easy to forget how lonely her apartment seemed.

She lifted Ella's small stack of pretty stationery, tied together with a lace ribbon, and tried not to regret leaving. Tried not to miss Alex. She thought of the enigmatic man she'd met. Of how she'd so immediately been drawn to him in a way she'd never experienced before. Yes, he was charismatic, intelligent, spectacular to look at, but it had been much more than that, much deeper.

Much as she would have liked to deny it, she'd been hopelessly attracted. It scared her to death, as little else had. For an attraction meant an attachment, and she'd never been good at that.

Hopefully, she'd soon forget Alex and his mesmerizing smile. Surely he'd easily forget her.

The phone rang, startling her. No one would call her this late on a Sunday. Confident the machine would pick it up, she relaxed back with Ella's letters and ignored it.

"Nicole, this is Alex."

Nicole jumped and stared at her machine in surprise.

"I know, you didn't give me your number," he said in his deep, sure voice that would forever remind her of the mountains of Sunrise Valley. "But you're listed."

A little laugh escaped her at the irony and humor in his voice, and she found herself grinning ridiculously.

"I just wanted to make sure you got home okay. We didn't get a chance to say good-bye—"

She'd never know what made her pick up the phone. "Hello?" she said quickly, rolling her eyes at the breathiness in her voice. "I'm here."

"Good." She felt his smile, and it warmed her. "You didn't have any problems with your car?"

"Of course not."

"I know." He laughed at her defensive tone. "It was just an excuse to call. You okay?"

"Of course."

"You ran off."

Why was her heart racing? "I didn't." Because her legs shook, she dropped to the couch.

"You did."

She pressed a hand against her quivering stomach muscles. "Okay, I did. I thought it would be different. It's so embarrassing, really."

"No. You tried."

He'd called. He cared. And the small glorious feeling she'd gotten at the first sound of his voice grew. "The sad thing is," she admitted, shocking herself by telling him, "I really liked it there."

"You'd have to be deaf, blind, and stupid not to." He paused, then his voice turned deep and husky. "Come back, Nicole."

For a minute she actually felt as if she were back in

the woods, standing next to him, skipping rocks across the lake. It made a tempting picture. "I gotta go, Alex."

"Think about it," he said softly. "I'll call again."

"Why?" she asked before she could stop herself.

"Because I like you." So simple. "And you like me too."

Cocky, yes, but it was true enough to have her smiling. "Good-bye, Alex."

She sat hugging the phone for long minutes after they'd hung up. *He'd called.*

Which was more than she could say for any member of her family. Carefully, she untied the ribbon on the letters in her hand and opened the first of three pale pink envelopes.

Dear Candy,

I miss you terribly! Today I made a will naming you legal guardian, just in case something were to happen to me and John. No one has to know, Candy, especially Mother. But it had to be done, you know it as well as I do.

Everything is fine, I promise. Nicole is beautiful. But I feel so much better knowing I've taken care of her. I hope you feel that way too.

Send my love to Ted and tell him I miss him too. I love you,

Ella

Nicole let out the breath she'd been holding very slowly. Her mother had thought she was beautiful. She closed her eyes, trying to recapture the bond they must have shared for their brief week together. But, of course, she couldn't.

What had happened to that will? And why hadn't

Candy mentioned this letter when they'd talked in the attic? She opened the next envelope and pulled out a picture of a young Ella, Candy, and Ted, sitting on a tree stump, their arms wrapped around each other and grinning at the unseen photographer. The second picture was of her father and mother, cradling her as an infant. She stared at the most beautiful picture she'd ever seen for long minutes, sorrow and unrequited love overwhelming her.

The last envelope was dated two days after the first letter and it contained a very short note from Ella to Ted. She wanted him to contact her regarding a complication to some medical problem she'd had.

What problem? Nicole wondered, sitting back on her couch. Had she been sick?

She found she had more questions now than she had before she'd gone to Sunrise Valley. Her family had not been there for her as she'd expected. But still, she deserved answers. She wanted to go back.

But what about when they disappointed and hurt her with their lies? She'd be all alone. No, she corrected, remembering Alex and his expressive, caring eyes. Remembering, too, how he seemed to understand her, even when she didn't understand herself. *Come back*, he'd said.

She wouldn't be alone at all, unless she wanted to be.

Three weeks later Nicole staggered up her apartment stairs, weighted down by gifts from her students. Teary-eyed, as she always was on the last day of school, she missed the deliveryman standing with a basket of wild flowers.

"Nicole Sanders?"

She jumped and stared at him. "Yes."

"Delivery," he said, thrusting out the basket. "Sign here."

Nicole managed to get into her apartment without dumping everything, and set the flowers on her table. No one had ever sent her flowers.

Slowly, she opened the envelope, enjoying the fresh scent filling her apartment. It reminded her of the woods in Sunrise Valley. Then a flat, smooth pebble fell out into her hands. The card read, *Yesterday on the lake I beat your record. Better come back and try again. Alex.*

A sound of amazement escaped her, right before her face split into a grin. Fool, she told herself, falling for the oldest trick in the book. Flowers. But she inhaled deeply and kept grinning.

Her phone rang less than a half hour later.

"School's out," he said simply.

"Yes," she said, immediately breathless just from the sound of his voice. "Alex . . . you know I can't do this, flattering as it is."

"Can't do what?"

"Can't . . ." She felt ridiculous. He hadn't asked her for a single thing.

"Nicole," he said gently, "just come back. Not for me, not for your family. Just for yourself."

"I am." Surprised, she sank to a chair. Yet it was true. She did want to go back. *For herself.* "But—"

"Don't fret," he told her. "I'm not going to push you."

"Good," she said firmly. "Because I'm coming back for that job. And some answers. That's it."

"But you'll stay the summer?"

"I won't back out and leave you stranded, if that's what you mean."

"You know it's not. See you soon, Nicole."

Nicole hung up and glanced at the three pictures of her family she'd framed and set on her mantel.

Yes, she was going back to Sunrise Valley. For answers. For a well-deserved break from the city. She remembered how Alex's smile had rendered her stupid, and knew she hadn't cured that problem yet either. Still, she was going back.

And she'd be lying if she said Alex didn't have anything to do with it.

FIVE

The Wilson House looked exactly as welcoming as Nicole remembered. More at ease than she wanted to be, Nicole walked down the hall, past the kitchen, toward Susan's office. The sharp voices told her exactly what she'd find.

Alex, Brad, and Susan stood around the large, neat desk, the air crackling with tension. Brad's hands were shoved in his pockets, and he was frowning in a way Nicole recognized as defensive. Susan, looking as cool and collected as always, had her arms crossed, her lips tight. Her foot tapped impatiently.

Only Alex looked amused.

Nicole stepped into the room. "You guys at it again?"

"Nicole!" both Susan and Brad said at once, each taking their turn at hugging her.

She endured the physical connection because it felt nice, but she had to forcibly remind herself this wasn't a social visit. A flurry of questions from Susan and Brad distracted Nicole briefly, though she remained all too aware of the silent Alex. He stood quietly next to her, and though he appeared completely relaxed, Nicole knew better. She could sense the underlying tension shimmering through him and wondered, whether it stemmed from her presence, or from the conversation she'd interrupted.

When she dared a direct look, his warm and appraising gaze met hers. No, she thought, her breath stuck in her throat, she doubted that look of his had anything to do with either of her cousins. It seemed all for her.

"Nicole." His expressive eyes leaped with hidden emotions. "Hello. Again."

"Hello." In her pocket, she fingered the pebble he'd sent her. "I had some . . . unfinished business."

The flare in his eyes came so quick and so hot, Nicole thought she'd imagined it. No one had ever looked at her that way, with so much longing and hunger. In a move that startled her as much as her cousins, he lifted her hand to his lips and kissed her fingers, watching her over them. "Well, for whatever reason, I'm glad you're here."

Someone gasped, and Nicole was reasonably certain it wasn't her. It couldn't have been, she still couldn't breathe.

"Dinner?" he asked, still holding her hand.

"I—"

"Don't even think about intruding on her first night back," Susan said, her voice tight despite her smile. "I've waited so long to see her again."

"I'd like to talk to both Candy and Ted first," Nicole said softly.

"No problem," Brad said. "They'll come."

Nicole wondered at his complete faith in his father and aunt. What was it like to be able to depend on someone, no matter what? Once again, her hands were drawn to the pebble in her pocket and she risked a glance at Alex.

He met her look, unwaveringly. *You can depend on me,* he seemed to say. *No matter what.* She felt her lips curve in a small smile she hadn't planned.

Never losing eye contact, Alex touched her cheek before matching her smile. "You do what you have to do," he said in a voice for her ears alone. "I'll be around." Then he was gone.

The man had a way of walking, she noted, unable to help herself. All confident, masculine movement without a hint of ego or attitude. And if hearts could sigh in feminine response, hers did. But she knew what she had to do, and ruthlessly forced her mind to it. She had to confront her aunt and uncle.

But she never got the chance. Because, despite her phone calls, neither of them came that night. Or the next.

Alex drove in from town, grumbling to himself. His materials had been inexplicably delayed—again. He refused to believe it was another coincidence, but something much more sinister. And he couldn't wait to get his hands on whoever was doing this to him.

Turning off the highway toward his resort, he saw the solitary figure standing beneath the entry sign and knew instantly who it was. Already, he was beginning to know that body, crave it, dream of it.

He opened the passenger door, but at the obvious strain to Nicole's features, the smile froze on his face. "Want a lift?"

Still silent, she got in. He drove them past the resort,

convinced they both desperately needed a break. The narrow unpaved road took them into the woods until all that existed was themselves and the nature that surrounded them.

"Where are we going?"

He glanced at her, wondering at the deep sorrow he saw in her eyes. "We're almost there."

When he pulled into the small clearing before his house, she stiffened. "This is where you live."

"Yes."

He watched her appraise the fifty-year-old log cabin. With a deep breath, she got out.

They sat side by side on his porch in a wooden swing. Insects hummed, trees whistled softly in the wind. Though they didn't touch in any way, Alex could feel a current running between them as if they were. He gave her the time she seemed to need, and they sat quietly.

Eventually, she looked down at some papers in her hands, pausing as if coming to some decision, then thrust them at him. "These were Ella's."

He looked at her, then opened the letters. "I thought there wasn't any correspondence after she left."

"That's the story," she said flatly.

He read them quickly, feeling the anger build for her. "Looks as if there's some inconsistencies, wouldn't you say?"

"Candy and Ted won't come to see me."

"Then we'll have to go to them."

"We?"

"Yeah," he said softly, reaching for her hand, hating the defeat he saw in her face. "*We.* Unless you'd rather go alone."

"I don't intend to stay."

His eyes stayed on hers, tough and unrelenting.

"Don't run away, Nicole. Don't disappoint yourself . . . or me," he said, deliberately challenging her.

"Dammit, you know nothing about this. Or me."

"This is too important," he insisted. He hadn't wanted her hurt, but it was too late for that. Now all he could do was help her heal. "Unless, of course, your life is rich enough with your other family that you don't feel the burning need to get to the bottom of this."

She made a sound and turned away. "I have no other family."

"Who did you live with growing up?"

"Foster homes." Her legs swung back and forth now, venting pent-up energy. "Twelve of them."

"*Twelve?*" He nearly choked on the word. Good lord, no wonder. So many things about her suddenly made sense. Her almost desperate need to get along with her family, her deep-rooted need to belong. Her loneliness. He glanced at her dispirited profile, at her bunched, coiled muscles, and he experienced a sudden surge of protectiveness and a need to help her. "Nicole, I'm sorry."

She sat ramrod straight, her arms crossed over her chest, refusing to look at him. "I don't want your pity, dammit."

"I don't—" He sighed and turned her to face him. "Nicole, I care about you." He could see the doubt in her eyes, and he ached a little for this woman who hadn't known the kind of family love he had. "I do. It has nothing to do with pity. *Nothing,*" he repeated firmly, cupping her face. They both jolted at the physical connection, and he knew by the confusion in her eyes that he'd made his point.

"Let's go get your answers. You deserve them."

She relaxed a little. "I do, don't I?"

He smiled and reached for her hand. "Ready to take them on?"

"Yeah." And she rewarded him with a rare, warm smile. Then she shivered in the cool shade.

"Come inside first, I'll get you a sweater." He opened his front door, then glanced around self-consciously, wondering if he'd remembered to pick up his clothes and do the dishes. By some miracle, he had.

She looked at the rustic interior, the wooden furniture, the haphazardly tossed throw rugs. "It's lovely," she said as he dashed up the steps to grab her a heavy cardigan sweater from his room.

But when he came back down, the living room was empty. He found her at the front door, one hand gripping the knob with white knuckles. She looked pale, shaken, and panic-stricken, and he realized with a start that she'd been about to bolt out the door. Without him.

"Nicole?" He stepped closer and her head flew up, her eyes wide. She yanked her hand from the door and put it behind her back. He pretended not to notice, but had the feeling if he so much as moved, she'd bolt. "Come here," he said quietly, and held out the sweater.

She looked like a doe caught in the headlights, but she came. "I'm going to have all your jackets before I leave." Her voice shook.

For some reason, his stomach quivered with nerves as well. "They look good on you." He stepped behind her and held the sweater out for her at the same moment that she whirled to take the garment. He found himself with her practically in his arms. Tossing the sweater around her shoulders, he inhaled the soft, flowery scent of her, felt her breath on his neck.

She stood stone-still, clenching the letters between them.

Alex's heart picked up speed as she slowly tipped her head up, her expression intent. He knew it matched his own. He rested his hand on the small of her back, the other came up to touch her face. But it wasn't enough, so he cupped her cheek, using his thumb to trail the curve of her lower lip.

"Alex," she whispered. "I haven't the foggiest idea what I'm doing."

She looked terrified of him. Tenderness, such as he'd never known, overcame him. "We'll just take it slow," he promised, knowing that was a promise that would kill him. She still trembled, and he paused, looking down worriedly at her. "You okay?"

"Yes . . . no," she corrected, unable to think, much less respond. Being with him did something to her insides that she didn't trust. But just his touch pushed some of her loneliness to another place, a place where it couldn't reach her. Slow, hot fingers traced her neck, and a tremor racked her body, along with a slow burn that started in the pit of her belly. The warmth and tenderness in his gaze touched her more than she wanted to admit.

"Let me help," he whispered, then his lips settled on hers in a soft, sweet kiss. The delicious heat only he could cause spread, and he tightened his arms around her, pulling her close.

Nicole let him deepen the kiss, knowing he offered compassion, companionship, and best of all, escape from the despair. She dropped the packet of letters. When he started to pull back, she threw her arms around his neck. "More," she whispered. "Please, Alex. More."

With a growl deep in his throat, he obliged her, giving her a hot, devouring kiss that took absolute possession. His tongue slid over hers in a way that brought erotic things to mind, and she never wanted it to stop. Then she discovered that by rubbing against him, she could wring a moan of approval from him that so thrilled her, she did it again and again just to hear him.

The doorbell rang, and Nicole lurched out of his arms. Alex cursed softly, and they both stood there, staring at each other, breathing heavily.

When it rang again, Nicole blinked and focused. Had she *really* begged him to kiss her? Self-consciously, she raised a hand to her lips, then dropped down to pick up the forgotten letters.

Alex opened the door to Candy, whose surprise turned to relief. "Nicole, I was looking for you. I started to worry. No one could find you." She rambled on nervously. "Your car's at the inn, so we knew you were on foot and . . ." Her voice faded anxiously away as neither Nicole nor Alex moved.

"You shouldn't have worried," Nicole said.

Candy's auburn hair shimmered beneath the daylight, matching Nicole's. "I couldn't help it."

"I can take care of myself."

Candy glanced at Alex, then back to Nicole. "I can see that. Is everything all right?"

After two days of trying to reach Candy and Ted, Nicole didn't want her concern. "I've been trying to get ahold of you."

"I just got back in town. I came as soon as I got your message."

"Come in, Candy," Alex suggested, moving aside. "You can talk here. I'll get drinks."

Nicole fingered the letters in her hands and sat across from Candy on the sofa. Feeling awkward, she busied herself by staring at the family pictures Alex had everywhere.

Candy glanced around. "I don't think I've been here since Alex's broken engagement."

"Engagement?" Nicole whispered weakly.

Candy looked at her strangely, then sighed. "I shouldn't have said anything. She left him a long time ago."

She left him. Nicole wondered if he still thought about her.

"Nicole, what are those?" Candy asked suddenly, her eyes riveted on the letters in Nicole's hands.

Hating this, as she did all confrontations, Nicole had to take a deep breath. "These are the letters that Ella wrote to you after she left town."

Candy shook her head. "No. That's impossible. She never sent me any letters, though I wish to God she had."

"I found them in the box you gave me in Ted's attic. They're addressed to you, they're postmarked . . . and opened."

"My mother must have gotten them," Candy said grimly. She flipped through them slowly, silently.

Alex came into the room, sat next to Nicole, and gently squeezed her hand. Even now she felt that sharp jolt of attraction, as she did whenever he touched her.

Finally Candy said, "I can't believe she kept them from me. Ted must never have seen them either."

"They were in his attic."

"That doesn't mean anything." Candy's eyes were glued to the letters. "Imagine how betrayed she must have felt that we didn't get back to her."

Nicole didn't have to imagine. She knew firsthand what that kind of pain was like and what it could do to a person. The pain of abandonment, of feeling unloved . . . it could destroy.

"What happened to the will?" Alex asked.

Candy shook her head. "As far as I know, there wasn't one."

"What about her health? What was wrong with her?" Nicole asked.

Candy's gaze dropped. "I know she had some female complications after . . . your birth." She jumped up. "I want to tell Brad and Susan I found you, they'll be worried." She smiled, a bit too brightly. "Susan told me you're working, doing some bookkeeping for the inn. I—I'm glad you're staying." Whispering her good-bye, she slipped through the door.

In the deep silence that followed her departure, Nicole sighed. "I hate this," she said, standing. She craved order in her life. In a world that had constantly shifted the rug from beneath her feet, she depended on it.

Alex reached for her as she walked to the door. "Don't give up, Nicole."

God, his eyes were deep. The slate gray should have seemed cold, but it was the opposite—warm, intense, and full of emotion she couldn't handle. "Alex, I can't . . . we can't do this now."

"Okay," he said agreeably, his eyes shining with humor as he softened his hold on her. "What can't we do?"

She looked at him in dismay, then realized by the dangerous amusement in his eyes that he was teasing her. "We can't have this . . . *thing* between us. It won't work. I don't even know who I am."

His humor vanished. "What's between us is the one thing that will always work, Nicole. No matter where you came from or who you are."

She studied the wood floor. "What if I don't want it?"

He tilted her chin up and stared into her eyes.

"That's better." He smiled as his gaze roamed her face. "You have the most incredibly expressive eyes, Nicole. They tell me everything, even when you're lying."

"I'm not." She panicked. She wasn't good at this. "I need to go, Alex. I have work to do."

"I know." He cupped her face with both hands now, making breathing difficult, because for some reason, she liked when he touched her. "Nicole, I know your life hasn't been easy, or even enjoyable, but you're entitled to change that."

She closed her eyes to escape the onslaught of the most powerful attraction she'd ever felt.

"This *thing*, as you call it, between us, has a life of its own," he told her gently. "You can deny it, ignore it, even fight it." His fingers stroked her jaw and had her stomach fluttering, her knees weak. "But you can't make it go away, Nicole."

Her eyes flew open. "*It* doesn't exist."

"Doesn't it?" he murmured, lowering his head, his eyes on hers.

"Alex," she warned, pulling back an inch. "I have work."

"In a minute." Their bodies drifted together, their clothing whispered against each other. Denim to denim, cotton to cotton. Her eyes drifted closed as the warmth from within her spread outward, and once again the despair she held so dear faded in his embrace.

"I'm here for you, Nicole, because yes, we're friends." His lips brushed her jaw, her neck. "But there's far more to it than that."

"No." But she tipped her head, giving him better access, and just managed to bite back her moan when he closed his teeth over her earlobe.

"Yes," he whispered. And he kissed her until she couldn't remember why she didn't want to.

Then he let her go.

When Alex didn't make a move to see her over the next few days as she worked at the inn, Nicole told herself she felt only relief. He'd gotten the message, finally. She didn't want to start something between them.

"You've been working hard." Susan came into the office where Nicole sat, trying to reconcile the inn's checkbook. It'd been badly neglected. "I've been too chicken to ask how bad I screwed up. I've always hated bookkeeping."

"It shows," Nicole said with a little laugh. "But don't worry, I'm sure I can straighten it out." Lucky for everyone involved, she'd earned her way through college by bookkeeping. "But I wanted to ask you why the amount of yesterday's deposit doesn't match what the register shows as the day's total income. Who made the deposit?"

"Brad." Susan grew quiet, tapping a finger against her lip in thought. "Oh, I remember. We issued a credit. There were some problems."

"Three hundred dollars' worth?" Susan turned away, obviously a little embarrassed. Nicole took pity. "Next time, just issue a credit memo so there's a record and attach it to your register. You've got to account for it."

"Okay. We're awful at this." She let out a little smile. "And Alex wants those books ready by the end of the month so he can see where we're at. Thank God you're here, or he'd have come and done them himself. We all know how much fun that would have been."

Nicole laughed at the mock horror on her face. "He's not *that* bad."

"No?" Susan watched her thoughtfully. "I guess that depends on your perspective."

"He's been good to you, hasn't he?" Nicole asked. She knew Alex owned the land and the inn that Susan leased. She knew also that Alex seemed to have a lot of patience and understanding in helping her cousins keep the business that should have reverted back to him when they failed to continue to pay on their lease.

"He's been fair," Susan said diplomatically.

Judging by the tension in her face, Nicole figured it was another subject better off dropped.

"Hey, girls." Brad swaggered in, looking proud of himself.

Susan whirled on him in a flash. "Where have you been? I needed you this morning."

He spread his arms wide, his warm eyes brimming over with sincerity. And a redness that said he hadn't slept. "Sorry."

Susan glanced down at his rumpled clothing and made a sound of disgust. "You went to Reno again, didn't you? You've been out all night gambling, and I'm here with the inn overbooked. Thanks, Brad. Thanks a lot." She moved to the door.

Brad stopped her, his face filled with remorse. But when he opened his mouth, Susan wagged a finger in front of his face. "*Don't!* Don't you dare apologize." She lowered her voice and grabbed his arms. "Listen to me, Brad. We're going to lose this inn to Alex if you don't help me. I can't do it by myself." She sent Nicole a grateful glance. "*We* can't do it by ourselves."

Nicole knew a quick moment of unease. She wanted to help, but she didn't like the feeling she had that she'd just unwillingly taken sides against Alex. She might not want to be involved with the man, but that didn't mean she wanted to hurt him either.

Susan turned on Brad and jabbed him in the chest with her long, manicured nail. "Shape up, got it? We need you."

Brad smiled at Nicole. "She loves me."

Nicole had to laugh. Even she already knew, Brad wasn't a worker. "She must, to put up with you. Brad, why don't you go do something you really like?"

He shrugged, sobering. "I don't know what I like."

"You'll figure it out," she said gently, feeling a tie with him she hadn't expected. He seemed like a lost soul, and that made them kindred spirits of sorts.

Until she'd come to Sunrise Valley she'd felt lost too. Even though there were still problems and questions to be resolved, Nicole had never felt so at home anywhere as she did there in the mountains. She was forced to wonder how much of that had to do with her family, and how much with Alex Coleman.

Then her heart stumbled a little as he walked into the office.

SIX

Alex watched Nicole's face register surprise, then pleasure before her customary caution set in. He nodded curtly as Brad and Susan made their way to the door, obviously eager to avoid him. "Hi," he said, drinking in the first sight of her he'd had in days.

"Hi." She fumbled about with things on her desk, then stood abruptly.

"Are you off somewhere?"

"Actually, yes, I—"

He took her hand and kissed her knuckles, rendering her speechless.

"Uh . . ."

He smiled against her hand, enjoying the jittery pulse he felt at her wrist, the way she lost her words when he made her flustered. She looked adorable. "I've missed you."

"Well, I've been right here," she said, slowly extracting her hand.

"I'd have come sooner, if I'd thought you wanted to see me."

"You'd have thought wrong," she said primly, making him laugh.

"I really have to go," she said, fingering her purse.

"You always do, when you're uncomfortable."

"Well, then, stop making me uncomfortable."

He bit back his smile since she seemed so serious. "I can't, if it means I have to stay away from you."

"Stop that," she said, stepping back. "Stop talking like we're . . . a thing."

He tried to contain his grin, so help him he did, but she caught it anyway and threw her hands up in exasperation. "There you go, laughing at me again. Glad I'm so amusing."

"You are, when you go denying the plain truth."

"I've got to go." She caught his look and gave him a half smile this time. "Well, I do. Really."

"Where to?"

"Ted's office." She opened her purse and held up the letters, her face suddenly shadowed by doubts and worries. "We haven't talked yet. He's been too busy."

Alex swallowed his anger at Ted, knowing it wouldn't do Nicole any good. Instead, he pushed the door open and took Nicole's hand. "Would you like company?"

She hesitated, then nodded, giving him a little smile that made his day.

They had to wait for Ted, which they did quietly. Nicole was grateful for Alex's silence as they sat in Ted's office, and for how he accepted hers. She'd never been good at small talk and couldn't have come up with any if she'd tried.

Ted, when he arrived, looked less than pleased to see

her again. He nodded to Alex. "It's nice that you're back, Nicole. It didn't go so well for us the first time, did it?"

"Not really."

"I know about the letters," Ted said, locking his fingers together on the desktop. "Candy told me."

Nicole experienced a quick spurt of irritation. "So you've been expecting me." Couldn't he have called her? "Have you seen them before?"

"Of course not." He rubbed his temples. "I had no idea she needed me. I would have gone to her."

His indignation seemed genuine. "What about her medical condition?" she asked.

"I know nothing about it."

Had he shifted slightly, had his eyes flickered away from hers, even briefly? Or had she imagined it? "I was thinking there'd have to be records, maybe a diary, that sort of thing."

Ted, looking grieved, sighed. "What difference could this possibly make after all this time?"

Emotion clogged her throat that he even had to ask. "What difference does it make?" Her breath whooshed out. "I have a hundred questions, have since I was old enough to understand that my mother was dead, yet you just take all that knowledge for granted. Did she love to read? Did she hate broccoli? Was she afraid of thunderstorms? . . . Did she want me?" Her voice cracked, and horrified at her outburst, she bit her lip. Alex reached for her hand, but she could no longer sit.

Pacing, she threw out the words that she had kept inside too long. "In school everyone traced their roots, their ancestors, their heritage. I got to do a book report." Understanding flickered in Alex's gaze, but she couldn't stop. "My foster parents could never help me," she continued, "and it hurt. I want to learn about her, Ted. Are you going to help me or not?"

Alex rose from his chair when Ted didn't speak, coming to her side. She actually felt his strength seep into her. She took her first deep breath since she'd started talking, and wondered how just a look from him could be so calming.

"I'm sorry," Ted said quietly. "I was thinking about old memories, and I suddenly realize that for you, they're not memories at all." He shook his head. "It's hard, Nicole. Ella was so dear to me and I loved her so much. When she left, I thought she dismissed us from her life, and now it turns out that wasn't the case at all."

"That should make it easier to remember her," she said softly. "And easier to look at me."

"Yes," he said. "Though I never should have doubted her in the first place. Nor taken it out on you."

"Your mother never should have meddled."

"She loved us, in her own way."

Nicole shuddered, thinking she was thankful not to have experienced that kind of love.

"I'm sorry," Ted said again, rising as his intercom buzzed. "I've got to go. But we'll talk."

Nicole wouldn't count on that. "Do you have any idea where Ella's medical records would be?" she asked.

Ted's eyes dropped to his mountain of paper work. "No."

He was lying, she'd bet money on it. And as quickly as it'd come, her relief faded to defeat.

Alex walked through the day-care center on his way to his office to find Krista sitting cross-legged in the middle of the empty floor, drawing up plans to decorate the center.

She frowned. "What's the matter?"

"Nothing."

Her eyes remained worried. But Alex knew that she wouldn't push. It wouldn't work anyway, and she well knew it. He was reputed to be the most stubborn Coleman alive. She held up her plans. "What do you think?"

"Okay."

"*Okay?*" she repeated, surprised. "You've been pushing and pushing to get this center ready to open. All you have to do is get the drywall inspection, spray the texture and paint, get the carpeting installed, and whamm-o . . . we're in business. And all you can say is *okay?*"

Alex leaned against the bare wall wearily. "What do you want me to say?"

She looked at him carefully. "How about, *it's perfect.* How about, *I scheduled an inspection today and got the okay to finish?*"

"It's perfect," he said dully, wishing for aspirin. "I scheduled an inspection."

"And?"

"And," he finished, "the only inspector for the entire county is tied up this week with important business and can't be disturbed."

"Ah," Krista said, understanding. "The marshal's at it again, huh?"

"Of course." He stalked the room, suddenly restless. His materials still hadn't arrived. Today he'd discovered the store had mysteriously lost his original order and he'd had to place it all over again. Another two-week delay.

"That's not all," Krista said, watching him. "What else?"

He looked at her. "What, are you turning psychic now too?"

She ignored that. "I went by the Wilson House on my way over here to pick up Susan's reports. Guess what I found?"

He had a good idea since his sister didn't miss much.

"I met the new cousin. Natalie?" She sent him a sly look.

"Nicole."

"Oh," she said slowly, nodding. "Nicole. She's pretty."

"Isn't she?" Candy stood in the doorway. She smiled at Alex. "I left my résumé on Krista's desk."

"You didn't have to do that," he said. "I already hired you as the center's director. Twenty years as the best teacher in the county was good enough for me."

"With everything my niece and nephew have put you through in the past few years, I wasn't sure this would be a good idea," Candy admitted. "But I really would love to work here."

"The other isn't your problem," Alex told her. "We can keep the two separate."

Candy looked at him thoughtfully. "Maybe so. Maybe now that Nicole is running the books over at the inn, things will go more smoothly."

"They should."

"She's quite good."

The underlying tension in her words was unmistakable. She was curious about his relationship with her niece, yet was too polite to ask. Krista watched, her ears pricking up in interest.

"Yes," Alex agreed. "She's good. I got my first

monthly statement yesterday. The first I've gotten all year."

Candy met his eyes directly. "I don't want her hurt, Alex."

He thought of how her family had already done so. "Believe me, I'm the last one you have to worry about."

Nicole ran a total on the adding machine, frowned, tore out the paper, and started again. She hit the total button, peered at the third answer she'd gotten in as many minutes, and cursed in a very unladylike way. She'd been trying to reconcile the inn's checkbook for two days.

"I didn't know you wore glasses."

She jumped at the sound of Alex's deep voice and self-consciously yanked the wire-framed glasses off. He stood in the doorway, looking lean, fit, and tanned. And far too gorgeous for her comfort. His dark hair was pushed back on his forehead by his sunglasses, emphasizing his rugged face. Those black jeans of his hugged endless legs, and his work shirt stretched tight over broad, sinewy shoulders and arms. "I didn't see you there," she said, ignoring the little leap her heart made at the sight of him.

She'd convinced herself that she had no reason to panic about her unexplained reaction to him. At the end of summer she'd happily go back to her city, and he'd just as happily remain here, on the mountain, where he belonged.

Nothing permanent, and no one hurt.

His gaze didn't leave her face as he moved into the room. "You look good in glasses."

"I look," she corrected knowingly, "like a nerdish bookworm."

He laughed. "Not quite." Sensuous seemed more like it. She wore a brilliant emerald sundress that was cut up to the neck but hugged those soft curves nicely. Her thick auburn hair was piled on top of her head, precariously balanced with a clip, but a few tendrils had escaped to curl about her face. "You look sexy."

"I have work to do," she said in a haughty tone that said *keep back*, but she blushed, giving herself away.

"I like it when you do that."

She wouldn't look at him. "Do what?"

He couldn't resist playing with a loose curl of her lovely hair. "Get all annoyed and talk like a prim schoolgirl." He was beginning to understand that it was her defense against him getting too close. He wondered if she really thought it would make him turn away from her.

She slapped at his hand, then worked fervently at the adding machine, trying to ignore him when he sat on the corner of her desk.

"It's a mess in here, isn't it?" he asked sympathetically.

"An absolute disgrace," she mumbled around the pencil she held in her teeth. She flipped papers around, searching for something, muttering to herself. Finally, she removed the pencil, wrote something down, and then looked at him impatiently. "Did you want something?"

Yeah, he wanted something all right. *Her*. But he also wanted to banish the lingering fear she still felt of him. "Learn anything new about Ella?"

She sighed and shoved the papers in front of her away. "No."

"You've got to push it, Nicole. Or you'll never be free for other things."

"What other things?"

Leaning close, he gave her a long, thorough kiss. "That."

Nicole drew back first, looking dazed. He couldn't blame her—after a gut-wrenching kiss such as that, he hardly knew his own name.

Her chair squeaked as she rose. As she started past him he put his hands on her hips and pulled her between his thighs. She let him, then jolted back, staring at him wide-eyed.

He laughed and grabbed for her. "It's just a hard-on, Nicole. Nothing to run from." He grinned. "Besides, you caused it."

"Well, I didn't mean to," she told him primly, crossing her arms between them. "So stop it."

He was still laughing when he took her mouth again. With his hands, he coaxed her stiff body as he spread kisses over her face, her neck, whatever he could reach. And one by one, her rigid muscles let go, until she leaned into him. Slowly, her arms rose up around his neck. And when he nipped at her throat, she made a catchy little sound that spread desire through him like wildfire.

This time when she pulled back, she put a hand to her own chest. "*Wow.*"

"Yeah." He gave her another soft kiss. "Wow."

"I've got to tell you," she said shakily, holding him off. "Humbling as it is to admit, that made my knees weak." Bonelessly, she slid back into her chair. "You're going to have to go away now. I need to think. And I can't do that with you looking at me."

He could look at her all day. "Do you analyze everything, Nicole?"

"Yes." She looked right at him. "I do. I've told you before, this isn't my kind of thing. Please, I need you to respect that."

He wanted to. He really did. "How can you walk away from this?" he asked her in a low, urgent voice. "When it's as strong as it is?"

"Easily." She wouldn't look at him. "Don't push me on this, Alex. It doesn't sit well with me."

He shook his head at her stubbornness, but gave in. Time, he reminded himself. And care. She needed lots of both. Luckily, he was a patient man.

Nicole felt a twinge of guilt when she saw Ted's crowded waiting room, but she was going to burst if she didn't find out more about Ella.

Just when they'd gotten past the banalities, his intercom buzzed. Casually, he pulled out a thick ring of keys from his pocket and dropped them on his desk. "I'm sorry, but I may be a few minutes. Feel free to wait."

Nicole eyed the full wall of file cabinets thoughtfully. Then the big fat ring of keys on her uncle's desk. She could see the labels on the drawers of the files. Patients, patients, and more patients. Accounting. Business . . . *Personal.* The decision made itself. Ted had no less than three huge filing cabinets labeled PERSONAL, but she sifted through them as systematically and as quickly as she could, keeping one eye on the door. She found conference info, continuing-education info, even his car loan. She found insurance, business contacts, his contract for hire. But nothing on Ella.

With a sigh of frustration and a worried glance at the

door, she eyed the last cabinet. It was locked. Three long, nerve-racking minutes went by as she searched for the right key with fingers slippery with nerves. Finally she slid the first of four drawers open and fingered through the files. Nothing, and she began to panic. But finally, in the last drawer toward the back, she found what she was looking for. *Family Medical Records.*

With another nervous glance at the door, she flipped past names she didn't recognize. Then some she did. Susan, Brad . . . The last file was the one Ted claimed he didn't have. Ella's. She yanked it out and opened it in the middle. Two words stuck out.

She stared at the page, her eyes riveted to the telling words as blood roared in her ears. Her heart drummed a heavy, fast beat. Her skin turned clammy. No, not possible. *Please, no.*

Then she heard Ted's voice down the hall and knew he'd open that door and find her standing there like a nitwit, holding his keys and a file marked PERSONAL. So she did the first thing that popped into her head. She slipped the file beneath the sweater she wore over her dress and slid the drawer shut. Throwing the keys on his desk, she took a deep breath and strove for a casual look.

Ted came in, still talking over his shoulder. Then he apologized for the delay.

"Don't worry about it," she said, completely unnerved. Sweat pooled at the base of her spine. "You . . . didn't by any chance find anything else of my mother's to show me, did you?"

Her heart pounded as she gave him one last chance to be honest. "No, I'm sorry," he said with regret. "I have nothing of your mother's here."

She nodded, feeling the weight of his lie under her sweater, sticking to her skin. At the door, she turned and found Ted staring sightlessly at the filing cabinet, lost in thought. She swallowed her meaningless good-bye and left.

She drove to the spot on the lake where she first met Alex and took her first deep breath since she'd seen the file. But not even the late-afternoon sun could warm her chill. Nothing could. Opening the file, she read it slowly front to back. Then she raised her eyes to the rich blue water.

Ella had been in a car accident at age thirteen, and as a result of that accident, she'd been left unable to bear children. She'd had a complete hysterectomy.

There was no way around it. Ella could not possibly have been her birth mother.

SEVEN

Nicole drove directly to a pay phone and called the county registry office for her birth certificate. Funny as it seemed, she'd never seen it before. She'd never needed it. Certainly, she'd never had any reason to think Ella wasn't her birth mother.

Ted must know. So would Candy. Did Brad and Susan? Could she be the only one *not* to know? God, that hurt. Once again, she didn't belong, and she never had. How many times had this happened to her? How many times had she gotten placed with a family she thought she could finally like, only to be transferred to another?

The registry office had already closed. Now she'd have to wait until morning. The sky darkened from pale blue to a deep purple while she sat in her car, numb. When the moon rose, she started her car, driving mindlessly over the curving roads.

She considered the possibility of Ted discovering his missing file. Then considered that she owed them no explanation at all. Two minutes later she was on the highway headed straight for San Francisco. *Forget them.*

Just forget them all. But then she glanced down and saw the black material of Alex's jacket. The one he'd given her on that first day at the lake. She'd just return it and *then* go home, she told herself, even as she turned around. Just see him one last time . . . maybe allow one last simple kiss.

Simple. Ha! Nothing about Alex was simple.

Vanity had her checking in the rearview mirror as she pulled up to his cabin. Disgust had her closing her eyes. She looked awful—which didn't matter since she was just going to drop the jacket off and go. *That was absolutely all she was going to do.*

The place was dark. A longing for him speared through her, even as she knew she'd never see him again. She walked around the back, intending to leave the jacket on his back porch, where it would be safe.

The night vibrated with the sound of crickets. The moon lit the way, the immense black sky twinkling brilliantly with thousands upon thousands of stars. Walking to the edge of the large wooden deck, Nicole gripped the railing and watched the breathtaking night, knowing she'd never see it from here again.

Her eyes stung, her chest ached. Then a board creaked behind her and she whirled as a tall, broad shadow emerged.

"Nicole?"

Alex. Her heart landed in her throat. She couldn't speak, not even when he came toward her, blocking out the view of the lovely valley far below. She stepped back, knowing if he touched her, even once, she'd break down. "Here," she said quickly, thrusting the jacket out. "I just wanted to bring it back."

He eyed her strangely as he took the garment and

tossed it onto a piece of patio furniture. "Thanks." He stepped closer. "You're not okay."

Hysterical laughter bubbled in her throat. "I don't think so," she said, shaking her head. "No. No, I'm really not."

In the dark of the night, his gray eyes gleamed like ice. The warmth and humor she'd come to depend on was gone. She'd hurt him earlier when she'd pushed him away from her.

"What's happened?" he asked, stopping a breath away, his hands in his pockets.

Nicole shifted uneasily under his intense gaze, knowing she looked unusually disheveled. Her hair had long since fallen free of its clip, and she hadn't bothered to repair it. Her eyes felt heavy with unshed tears, and she looked at him with all the caged-up yearning she suddenly felt. With fascination, she watched the ice in his eyes crack, replaced by a raw hunger that matched her own.

Without another word, he yanked her into his arms. She burrowed close, sighing with relief.

"What is it?" he murmured, his cheek against her hair.

She could feel the tension in him, hear the rough concern in his voice. She gripped him all the tighter for it, feeling the rock solidness of him beneath his shirt. He was comfort and security, and some stronger emotion that had always eluded her in the past, which didn't yet have a name.

"I just . . . wanted to see you," she whispered, and found that was the utter truth.

He nuzzled her neck with questing lips, and she closed her eyes. Then he nibbled her ear, turning her knees to Jell-O. Slowly, he bent his head until their lips nearly touched. His curved slightly, and the small, special smile warmed her as nothing else could have.

He kissed her then; a sweet, hot, wet kiss that had her despair receding within seconds. She could feel the heat within her, pushing away the remaining chill, and her body came alive, making her respond with a need she hadn't known existed. He wanted her too, she knew just how much the moment she pressed herself against his full, hard length.

"Nicole?" he whispered on a harsh sigh, his hands streaking over her.

She knew what he was asking, knew that this time there'd be no turning back. "Yes," she said shakily, her body straining against his as his thumbs teased the undersides of her breasts. A warm hand rose up, cupping her in his palm. She whispered a sigh and gave in to the unbearable ache, the delicious torment. Oh, she knew she should warn him now, tell him how inept she was, but it was so easy to close her eyes and let him take her. Then his fingers flickered over a taut nipple and there was no taking involved—she was giving, giving, giving.

His gaze met hers, burning hot. While their mouths clung, his fingers ran up her bare thigh, pulling up the hem of her sundress as they went.

"I didn't come for this," she managed, arching against his hand.

"No, but you want it as much as I do," he said a little roughly, thickly. "And I do want you, Nicole. So much." As he nibbled gently on her lower lip his fingers slipped under the lace edging of her panties.

She gasped when his fingers found her, dug her nails into his shoulders. "Alex—"

"You're so wet." His voice came low, gravelly, as he trailed warm lips down her neck. "So hot."

The heat grew within her, and she forgot to tell him she didn't know what she was doing. A fire raged deep in the pit of her belly, and she'd never felt so out of control in her life. Madly, she dug her nails in deeper, knowing she'd fall if he let go of her. "Alex . . ."

His mouth returned to hers, feasting on it while his fingers caressed her in sync with his tongue, making her writhe against him, completely mindless. Her legs gave out, and he followed her down onto the large, plush lounge behind them. Sinking into its softness, she reached for him, helping him peel off first her clothes, then his.

A breeze caressed her hot skin, the soft wind stirring the branches like music. Gently, he gathered her against his hard, demanding body. Nicole closed her eyes against the suddenness of it, the shock of his warm, nude body layered on hers reminding her to be stiff and awkward. He'd retreat now, she thought, just as soon as he realized what a bungling idiot she could be.

But he didn't. When he kissed her possessively, thoroughly, she realized reality had no place on that lounge. He was a masterful lover, his hands gliding tirelessly down her sides, her legs, her arms, slowly and deliberately, making her move against him, needing him somehow to ease the unbearable tension within her. She was humiliatingly close to begging, but for what, she had absolutely no idea. She'd never felt this . . . insane, crazed need. She'd never felt anything like it.

Those talented fingers played over her, caressing and tingling, and she wept with longing, her hands fisted in the cushions at her sides. Then he bent over her, drew a nipple into his wet, hot mouth. She nearly came right off the lounge. Unprying one of her hands from the cushion, he placed it against his chest so that she could feel the fierce pounding of his heart.

"Touch me," he whispered gruffly, moaning when she did.

Gaining courage, she lifted her other hand and ran them both over the corded strength of him, down over his flexed abdomen.

But then his fingers found the slippery center of her, and he swallowed her gasping cry, slowly rubbing her until she couldn't stand it. Her hands fell away from him limply. "Alex . . ." She lifted her hips insistently, the wonderful friction his fingers caused driving her mad. "Now."

"No, love," he murmured huskily. "We have plenty of time." And he continued his slow, unhurried torture as she strained and bucked beneath him, racing toward the unknown. Then, when her legs had started to quiver with tension, he lifted his head, holding her stare, and purposely pinched her lightly between his fingers. She exploded, racked by tremor after tremor as her climax ripped through her.

Eventually, she managed to open her eyes, surprised to see she still lay on the lounge under the moonlit sky. So that's what it felt like. She grinned. It was incredible, and she wanted more.

"Something funny?"

"I liked that," she said with some amazement. "I really liked it."

He let out a muffled laugh that might have been a groan. She touched his chest in marvel at what he'd done to her, then noticed the naked, fierce longing still written on his face. *His turn.* Running her hands down the length of his flat stomach, she hesitated, unsure of her next move. Could she just . . . touch him?

He didn't even breathe. When she encircled him with shaking fingers he moaned, then kissed her hard, moving her hands away to pin her to the mattress beneath him.

"Did I do that wrong?" she asked, closing her eyes on the humiliation.

"God, no," he rasped, his body hovering over hers. "Are you kidding?"

"You—you took my hands away from you. So I thought—" Oh, God, why didn't he just kiss her again to shut her up?

He tilted her head up and waited until she opened her eyes. His sparkled with something more than passion, and she was deathly afraid it was humor, but his voice remained low, sexy, and *very* serious. "I was hoping to make this last more than three seconds, which is all it would take if you keep touching me."

She opened her mouth. "Oh. You mean, I . . . that I—" She hesitated, but her newfound power overruled the lingering embarrassment. *She had to know.* "*I* could make you . . . lose control?"

Laughing, he dropped his forehead to hers. "Nicole, this isn't a good time to make me laugh." Shifting over her, he entwined their legs. "Just seeing you does things to me. Seeing you smile, hearing your lovely laugh, feeling your gorgeous body tremble beneath mine, having your hands on me." He kissed her. "I've pictured making love to you; seen your sweet body sprawled out, your eyes dark with passion, your lips wet from my kisses. I've pictured it, Nicole, how you'll look at me, how you'll make those little sounds that tell me how turned on you are, how we'll ravish each other. I've imagined how it'll feel to be hard, inside you, how hot and wet you'll be for me. . . . God, I want you so much."

"Oh," she breathed, so caught up in his erotic words, she couldn't function. She moved experimentally beneath him, staring in wonder when he groaned again.

"I get hard just looking at you, Nicole. Do you feel me? Can you feel how hard I am now?" He twisted his hips. "Can you?"

She nodded and clutched at him as she was swept under the pool of longing again. "Yes. I want you too, Alex. Please, now."

He gathered her face in his hands, nudged her thighs apart with his and entered her. She cried out as the heat consumed her, and he gathered her tight against him, moaning her name when she lifted her hips to give him better access. Again, he thrust full-length into her, wrenching another cry from her throat.

As he moved within her he lowered his head, nuzzling at a breast, drawing her aching nipple into his mouth, making her muscles tighten again. Still, he kept the rhythm, speeding up as she cried out with the mounting tension. Without warning, another earth-shattering release staggered her.

Wow, she thought, even as Alex went rigid in her arms, that was dazzling. And scary as hell.

When Alex could breathe again, he lifted his head and looked down into Nicole's face. The pulse at the base of her neck still leaped erratically, and he placed a kiss there, watching as her amber eyes fluttered open.

The way they slammed shut immediately caused him to frown. He rolled to his side to ease his weight off her, but she clutched at his shoulders and made a soft sound of what he thought might be protest. Pulling her close, he said quietly, "I'm not going anywhere."

But *she* was, he thought, sure that one of two things was about to happen. Either Nicole would bolt from him in fear of the feelings he'd drawn from her, or she would wrap her arms around him and demand her third orgasm. Pure ego had him grinning with satisfaction that he'd been the first to bring her to climax, but the smile faded quickly when he realized why. She'd never trusted anyone before. Before him. He was still lost in the joy of that trust when she pushed away from him and sat straight up.

He reached for her. "Nicole—"

"I'm sorry, I've . . . got to go."

"Now?"

"Yeah." She stood unsteadily, staring at the lounge as if she'd just realized what they'd done. She took a deep breath. "I'm not very good with this after thing, Alex. I don't know whether to leave, say thank you, or—" She pressed a hand to her mouth, looking confused.

He managed to stand up on his rubbery legs as she yanked on her panties. "They come off so much faster than they go back on," she muttered, nearly falling over as she fumbled with the inside-out sundress.

Taking her shoulders in his hands, he forced her to look at him, nearly swearing at the pain he saw pooled in her eyes. "Don't, Nicole." Gently, he pried her dress from her tense fingers and righted it for her, then helped her into it.

"It was just physical," she said stubbornly, bending her head so he could zip her. "Purely a physical reaction. That's all."

He let out a little laugh. "An explosion, more like." He turned her to face him. "But it was definitely more than physical."

"No."

She looked so terrified, he let it go, biting back the

need to tell her what they'd shared went far beyond the mutual pleasure of two bodies.

"We were stupid about it."

Alex tried to draw her close, but she pushed away. He studied her quietly as she struggled with her sandals. "I'm not going to give you any contagious diseases, if that's what you're worried about."

Her eyes were huge. "What if I get pregnant? My God, I teach sex education to kids half my age every day, and I just conveniently forgot every single rule because it suited me to do so."

Admittedly, it had been the first time he'd ever gotten so carried away as to forget a condom. And he still was shaking, but only because of how strong and true the emotions had been. "As unlikely as that is," he said calmly, "we'll deal with it." He tried to propel her back to the lounge to sit, but she jerked out of his arms.

"We'll *deal* with it?"

He didn't think now was a smart time to tell her that the idea of her having his child didn't disturb him in the least. He was only beginning to understand the depth of his feelings for her. "I only meant for you not to panic before it's necessary."

She shook her head, looking amazed. "I just never knew. . . ."

He knew exactly what she meant. "I think we should talk."

She stopped and looked at him sadly. For the first time that night he got a good, clear look at her face and the deep, weariness etched there. "I shouldn't have come, Alex. I'm so sorry."

"Don't be afraid of this."

That got her. "I'm not afraid." Scoffing lightly, she kicked at a fallen twig. "I just—" Her breath came out in one big sigh. "Okay, I'm afraid. A little. It was good, Alex, maybe too good." She looked up and must have caught his smile of satisfaction. With a little laugh, she backed away, her hands out. "Don't you dare come over here, Coleman. You look far too sure of yourself, and I'm not feeling . . . quite myself."

"I just want to kiss you," he said softly, his hands itching for her, his body hardening again at the thought.

"No." She backed up to the stairs of his deck, her little smile softening her words. "Not now, not yet. I'll just melt again."

"I made you melt?"

"You know that you did. Please, let me go."

Did he have a choice when she looked at him that way? As if she trusted him? "Go then, Nicole. Go while you still can."

When she'd gone, Alex sank to the lounge, which was still warm from their bodies. A falling star shot across the sky. *Just physical.* Like hell, he thought. Then he grimaced and shifted. But right now he would have joyfully settled for the physical aspect. Lying back, he forced his mind off Nicole's incredible body, off her wild response to him, and tried to concentrate on something else.

Nothing came to mind.

The cool night breeze on his bare skin reminded him he was still quite nude. Rising, he took himself upstairs, where sleep was a long time in coming.

By dawn, Alex was awake, his mind whirling. The previous night, before he'd taken Nicole into his arms and lost himself, he'd been sure she'd come to him for a reason, that something was the matter. Then he'd let her leave before he'd found out what. He'd kick himself for that later, but first he had to find her, had to reassure himself that she was okay.

He found her in the kitchen of the inn, alone and sipping from a mug. She took one look at him and ducked her head, concentrating on carefully stirring her tea. Unable to help himself, he moved close to kiss her, but since she kept her head averted, all he got was her temple. "Good morning," he murmured, patiently running his lips over whatever he could get, which happened to be her cheek.

She grunted noncommittally, but he took satisfaction in the way her hands trembled as he moved his mouth over her. Taking the cup from her, he set it down and caged her between the counter and his body. For a minute she sagged against him, all soft and eager woman, then she pushed away.

"Pretty friendly greeting, boss."

"Not nearly as friendly as I'd like," he murmured. But she moved her head when he would have landed a kiss on those kissable lips. Since she wouldn't kiss him, wouldn't touch him, and wouldn't look at him, he finally gave up. With a sigh, he slipped his hands in his pockets but didn't back away. She hated confrontations, he already knew that, but maybe forcing one was the only way to get to her.

"Last night we made love—yes, *love*," he stated firmly when she made a sound of protest. "And you got one thing right, Nicole. It was certainly physical, among other things. But now you can't even look me in the eye." He gave her a half smile that did nothing to erase the deep ache of worry that had settled in his gut. "It's enough to make a guy wonder if you still respect him."

"This is not a joke, Alex. Don't you dare treat it like one."

"Oh, believe me," he said, anger surfacing. "This isn't funny in the least. I don't know what demons were nipping at your heels last night, but I won't allow you to use me that way. It isn't fair to me and it isn't fair to you."

The urge to cry vanished, to be replaced by a deeper, uglier emotion. Pure anger. "*Demons?*" she sputtered. "*Use you?*" She shook her head. "I didn't use you. I just came by to . . ." To what? she thought desperately. "I just wanted . . . I didn't mean for us to—" She broke off in frustration. Hell, she *had* used him, and she felt sick over it.

"Didn't you?" His jaw clenched tight. "You may want to regret what happened now, but you came to *me* last night, Nicole. You came to me, and you were a willing partner in everything we did."

"Yes," she agreed, anger and embarrassment making her face heat uncontrollably. "You were a great lover, Alex. Does that make you feel better? Is that what this is about? You were the best I've ever had."

The way he looked at her, the way he seemed to see straight through her heart of hearts to her aching soul, drained the anger as quickly as it'd come. And she knew—he was right. She'd used him to help her forget her shocking news of the day before. "Oh, God," she whispered, closing her eyes and leaning back against the counter, thankful for its support. "You're right. I'm so sorry." She slid her hands over her face, then heard his soft, self-mocking curse.

Peeling her hands from her face, he gently pressed her head to his shoulder, closing his wonderful arms around her. "Nicole, stop it. This isn't some quick one-night stand—"

"That's exactly what it is." She grabbed fistfuls of his

shirt, and feeling needy, held on. "It can't happen again, Alex. Promise me."

"Can't do that," he said evenly. "But nothing's ever going to happen that you don't want. I *can* promise you that." She remained silent, and he laughed. "But that's the problem, isn't it? You're afraid you'll *want* to do it again."

Of course she was, but that wasn't what made her eyes spill over with hot, fast tears. The previous night she'd been able to push away what she'd discovered, but now, in the harsh light of the morning after, she could think of little else.

She was no one's daughter, no one's relative. She'd made love with the only close friend she'd ever had, and things could never be the same again. When the sob she'd been choking on escaped her, Alex's arms tightened.

"Oh, Nicole," he said softly, kissing the top of her head, her cheek. "Baby, don't." He ran his hands over her arms and back. "It's going to be okay."

She doubted it. But she needed to get to the recorder's office. With an effort, she let go of his warm, possessive embrace and forced a light smile. "I'll be okay. Really. It's just a combination of things. I've . . . got to go."

"All right," he said lightly, scooping up the keys she'd set on the counter.

"What are you doing?" she asked, tugging on her keys, panicked. "Let go."

"Do you trust me, Nicole?"

She looked into his stormy gray eyes. Trust him? She trusted no one. It was one of life's hard-learned lessons. But neither of them relinquished their hold on the keys.

"Do you, Nicole?" he asked softly.

Do it, a little voice inside her cried. *Just try it.* "It's hard," she whispered.

His little smile was bittersweet. "That's what makes it so valuable. Could you at least try?"

She'd never had much luck with trust. She couldn't even trust her own family, but somehow, she knew with Alex it would be different. The question was, did she trust herself? "I don't know. Maybe."

"Well, that's a start," he said, smoothing his thumb over her fingers that still gripped the keys. "Tell me what's wrong."

Admit that she belonged nowhere? That no one cared enough about her to be honest with her? "I can't."

"Promise you're not leaving?"

"I'm not going home."

"But you are leaving," he said flatly.

She had to do this alone, go to the recorder's office.

He studied her carefully. "Tell me."

Good. Anger. It made her strong. "Don't boss me, Alex. I've had enough of that to last a lifetime."

"I'm not," he said, with so much understanding in his eyes, she felt her throat tighten. His hands slipped around her waist, and her treacherous body leaned into him. "I care about you," he whispered, stroking her back and her emotions into oblivion. "Is that so hard to understand?"

His velvety voice sent a ripple of remembered pleasure through her body. "Yes."

"It shouldn't be," he chided gently. Then his lips closed over hers in a warm kiss that left her yearning, aching, wanting. And then, he was gone.

Ten minutes later she was showered and on her way.

She knew a brief pang of regret, knowing Alex would be both hurt and angry if he found out she'd left after she'd promised not to, but she couldn't help it. She had to do this—without him. She could deal with his expected anger, she had lots of experience with that. But the thought of hurting his feelings was tough to accept.

Yet she couldn't concentrate on what had happened between them, not when she had a bigger, hotter burning question.

Who the hell was she?

EIGHT

The county recorder's office didn't have Nicole's birth certificate, but they had a good reason for that. She'd been adopted at birth by Ella and John Sanders, and her records were sealed. She'd filled out the required paperwork to petition the state to open those records, but that could take months. In the meantime she had no idea who was listed as her birth mother on the certificate.

She was angry, hurt, and betrayed—a deadly combination for Nicole. She refused to budge from Sunrise Valley now, much as she would have liked to disappear. There was no doubt she belonged to this family—she looked just like them. Candy had never married, supposedly never had kids, but she couldn't be ruled out. Then there was Ted. Could she be his illegitimate daughter?

Susan came around the corner as Nicole entered the inn. Her worried expression brightened. "Nicole, I've been so worried. I thought—you look so tired. Are you all right?"

The exhaustion crept up now, as did hunger. "Just sleepy. I think I'll go rest."

"I'll see that no one disturbs you," Susan said with such purpose, it gave Nicole pause. "Alex came looking for you this morning."

The guilt wasn't unexpected, but the pang of regret was.

"Is everything really okay? I mean, if he's bothering you—"

"No," Nicole said quickly. "He's not. There's nothing to be concerned about." Again, she was reminded of the long-term implications one night of passion could have.

"That's good," Susan said, her shoulders relaxing. "Because he's . . . well, not exactly your type. And he's absolutely possessed by his resort. He's not a good catch, Nicole. Not the kind for the one-woman relationship you deserve."

"Oh," she said weakly. At the moment she was more worried about his certain anger over her lie than anything else. Besides, she wanted nothing to do with a committed relationship with him. Absolutely not. "I'm really fine."

Susan sighed and leaned dramatically on the stair railing. "Wish I could say the same."

"What's the matter?"

"You've seen the books."

Nicole took a deep breath and concentrated on not falling asleep right there on the steps. "I know you're behind on your payments to Alex, if that's what you mean. The inn itself has been doing well."

"I know, this isn't your concern." Susan gave her a sad smile. "But you're the only one I can talk to, and when I thought you'd left me, well . . ." She gave a little relieved laugh. "I'd really miss you."

The words meant far more to Nicole than she

wanted to admit. To be wanted, needed . . . it felt too good. But she still wouldn't say a word about her birth certificate until she held it in her hand. "I'm not going anywhere. And neither is the inn, even if you do owe Alex too much money. Can't you get a business loan?"

"Not with my credit." At Nicole's surprised glance, Susan self-consciously patted her hair. "I wasn't always as put together as I am now. I've made plenty of mistakes."

"Can't your dad help?"

"Not likely. He doesn't exactly trust my business sense. What I need is a rich relative. Maybe an inheritance."

"Someone would have to die for that," Nicole said so thoughtfully that Susan laughed.

"Yeah, I guess you're right. Darn it." She looked at Nicole. "Too bad you're not rich. You could buy out my boss and be my partner."

They both laughed, but Nicole paused. She did have a little money saved. Maybe instead of taking from this supposed family of hers, she could do something else. She could give. "I could help you out a little, Susan."

Her cousin's entire face lit up. "You would do that? For me?"

Surprised at how easy it'd been, and how good it felt, she nodded, smiling. After all, this woman could be her sister. "Yes, I'd do that. For you."

After, outside her room, she paused, one hand on the handle, her heart constricting.

At her feet lay a single, perfect rose.

Alex chose to forgo his office in favor of pounding nails, but even physical exhaustion couldn't get Nicole off his mind. She'd ditched him, though he shouldn't have been surprised.

In the end she hadn't trusted him, even a little. He should have listened to her, should have read the truth so evident in her eyes, but he hadn't wanted to believe he hadn't made any headway with her at all.

He should have known that the bond between them was tentative at best, at least for her. But he needed more—something of a shock, because usually at this point in a relationship, he felt smothered and confined. He felt the opposite now, and wanted more than anything to think Nicole could work through her basic mistrust and fear. But he was scared she couldn't.

Obviously, as she'd already done, it would be easier for her to run.

Nicole reconciled herself to the fact that she had at least a month wait before learning the truth about her birth. But she couldn't settle her thoughts so easily regarding Alex. She spread out the inn's accounts she'd taken to the veranda to balance, but could see nothing but those stormy gray eyes, could feel nothing but his warm, possessive arms around her. . . . She jumped when the man himself stepped out of her daydreams and onto the veranda, looking better than any man had a right to look.

She expected a show of temper. He confused her when instead, he smiled warmly, and with relief. "You're here."

"Yes."

"I thought you'd left. Gone home."

She could only shake her head, unable to tell him she had no home.

"Working hard?"

"Sort of." She squirmed, waiting for the questions and incriminations, braced for his anger. He just kept smiling. "Thanks for the rose," she said awkwardly. "It's lovely."

"*You're* lovely. It's good to see you, Nicole."

His eyes weren't filled with rage at all, but with something nearly as devastating. Tenderness. An unfamiliar tug of emotion stuck in her throat, and she shook her head against it, slapping both hands on her papers and rising. "All right, I can't stand it. Let's get it over with."

"Okay," he said easily. "Get what over with?"

So this was the way he wanted to play it. He'd make her say it. In her pocket, she fingered the smooth pebble he'd sent her all those weeks ago. "Go ahead," she told him, waving her hand and then turning away with her arms crossed over her chest. "Let's have it. Tell me how mad you are."

She nearly leaped out of her skin when his voice came from directly behind her. "Why would I be mad?"

She could feel his breath in her hair, the heat of his body so close to hers, but she refused to turn. His voice had been low, unbearably sexy, making her heart trip.

"What is this, Nicole?" Those strong hands touched her tense shoulders. "You're standing there as if you're awaiting sentencing."

She flinched, his choice of words slamming unhappy memories into her. Too many authority figures, she thought miserably. And she'd been moved around so much, she could never learn the rules fast enough.

"No, don't do that," he murmured, wrapping his hard, giving arms around her, bending to kiss her neck. "Don't stiffen up on me."

But she remained frozen in his arms, shaking.

And it left Alex struggling with his own emotions. He found she'd torn his heart open with just that small, involuntary movement. She'd actually been afraid of his possible anger. "Nicole," he said softly, still holding her tense body against him. "I'm not mad. You wanted to be alone and you tried to tell me, I just didn't listen. I'm sorry for that. I promise, I'll listen to you from now on. Just promise me one thing in return."

She hesitated, and he couldn't blame her. "What?"

He enjoyed the feeling of her petite body snuggled against his, but let her go to turn her around and see her face, keeping his hands on her arms. "Promise you won't ever expect the worst of me again. I think you must be used to being ignored, sent away, or worse." She tried to pull free, but he managed to continue gently holding her. "I would never do any of those things, Nicole. I swear it."

"I want you to let go of me."

"You got it." She backed away, her eyes shadowed with mistrust and confusion, and he tensed with a burning desire to seriously injure each and every person who had ever hurt her over the too many years she'd been on her own. He smiled what he hoped looked like an easy, carefree smile. "Want to go for a walk?"

She ignored that, still staring at him as though expecting him to turn on her. She'd been hurt too many times, and the knowledge filled him with rage.

"You're not mad," she repeated, obviously not convinced.

"Nope." He was, but not at her, and he shook with the struggle to hide it.

"I don't want to regret the other night because it was . . . wonderful," she said finally, the awe in her voice making him smile. "But it put ideas in your head about us that I can't handle right now."

He let his breath out slowly. That he understood didn't help. She was terrified of the feelings they brought out in each other. Hell, he was, too, but he still wanted her. "I told you I'd never push you to do anything you don't want to do. I meant it."

"But you want to do it again."

He laughed then, he couldn't help it. "Well, yes. Are you trying to tell me you don't?" She blushed beautifully.

"Because we're being honest, remember?" He smiled wickedly. "Go on, Nicole, tell me you don't ever want to make love again, and I'll have to believe you."

She looked away.

"Come on, tell me."

"Shut up," she said, making him laugh again. She might fear the emotions he caused her to feel, but he was certain now she didn't fear him.

Tipping her head back, she studied him. "So . . . we're still . . . whatever the hell we are?"

"What do you think?"

"I don't know. I'm not very good at this sort of thing."

She looked so uncertain, so damned vulnerable. "You're doing fine," he assured her. "And so are we." He took her hand, pleased when she didn't pull away. Slowly, gently, he pulled her slim body against him, sighing as he rested his chin on her head.

God, she was stubborn. But so was he. He wouldn't give up. He couldn't.

The inn remained busy. Full, it hummed with life. Nicole loved it. Having a lot of people around, she decided, was kind of nice. *Real* nice.

But then Candy came outside to where she sat, wearing that small, hesitant smile she always seemed to wear around Nicole. "Hi," she said. "Busy?"

"Not now." Nicole pushed her drink aside and struggled to relax. She'd decided not to confront Candy without a birth certificate for fear of more lies, but waiting was difficult.

"I just came from the resort," Candy said carefully, easing into a chair.

Her stomach tightened. "Oh?" She hadn't seen Alex in two days, and instead of the relief she'd expected, she felt a keen disappointment.

"It's official. I'm the new director of the day-care center." Candy lifted her hands. "I'm just so excited, I had to tell someone."

"Why not Susan?" Nicole asked quietly. "Or Ted? Or Brad?"

Candy's smile faded. "I wanted to tell you."

Candy had never sought her out before. "Well, I'm happy for you, it's a great position." Nicole played with her glass. "But I guess I can't figure out what made you tell me first."

Candy stood awkwardly. "I don't really know, Nicole. I guess I just wanted to share it with you." She walked to the door before pausing. "I realize we got off to a bad start, but I'd hoped to change that."

There had been a time, up until a few days earlier, when Nicole had wanted this more than anything. Now she simply didn't know what she wanted. "Why now?"

Candy looked at her in mute misery, as if she were desperately sorry but unable to fix things because she didn't know how, and something funny clicked inside Nicole. She recognized Candy's expression well enough—she'd perfected it herself. Was this her mother? "Wait. Don't go. I'm sorry." She sighed. "It's hard sometimes, Candy. I feel like an outsider, and it makes me question everyone's motive."

"I can understand that." Candy let go of the door and looked at her. "But I wish you wouldn't. The last thing I want is for you to feel like an outsider here."

"I can't help that," Nicole said with a little shrug. *I am an outsider here.* "There's too much between all of us for it to be any different."

"It doesn't have to be that way," Candy protested.

But Nicole saw no choice. No choice at all.

Alex dropped the phone back on its receiver, gaining no satisfaction from the crash it made. It'd happened again. This time his supplies had been delivered to the wrong place—two hundred and fifty miles away.

"Problems, darling?"

He groaned as Susan positively floated into his office and dropped gracefully into the chair opposite his desk, beaming cheerfully. "What's this?" he asked, glancing suspiciously at the check she dropped in front of him.

"This month's lease."

He didn't trust that elegant smile, or those cold eyes. "How did you get it?"

Her smile didn't quite reach her eyes. "You don't have much faith in me, do you?"

"You've yet to be honest with me." He watched her eyes darken with anger. "Come on, Susan, what gives? You've never been worried about what I thought of you before."

"You don't think so?"

He gave her a long look. "I know so."

"You're wrong," she said quietly, her expression strangely hurt and . . . genuine. "I've always cared about what you thought. That's one of my greatest problems."

He stared at her in surprise, wondering if this was her latest game. If so, it'd definitely thrown him for a loop. She came around the desk to face him. When she lifted a hand to his face, he scooted back, his scowl deepening. "Knock it off, Susan. We're not kids anymore. I'm immune to your charms this time."

She smiled. "You liked me well enough back then."

He thought of the trouble she'd caused him all those years before, the trouble she was still causing him. "Yeah, well, I learned my lesson. The hard way, remember?"

She lifted her perfectly curved brows. "You aren't going to claim I broke your heart. No one's done that and you know it."

He turned away, disgusted at the memories she evoked. "Just tell me how you got the damn money, Susan, and get out. I don't trust you."

She smiled at that. "My generous cousin helped me out."

He went cold all over. "Nicole?" The desk was between them now, and he leaned over it on two arms as anger vibrated through him. "I don't know how you've managed to fool such an intelligent woman, Susan. Probably by preying on her giving heart with this sympathetic family routine, but if you hurt her, I'll—"

Susan laughed. "You'll what?" Her amusement faded, to be replaced by a fierce protectiveness he recognized all too well. "The only person who underestimated me is you, Alex. You tried to take away the only thing that ever meant anything to me and I won't allow it."

"The inn?" He shook his head, saddened. "You were *never* interested in Nicole, were you? You read about her grandmother dying and you thought you had a rich relative."

"You don't think very highly of me."

"I try not to think of you period," he said. "But you're making it difficult."

Susan sniffed delicately. "Oh, fine. Be insulting. Just take the money, Alex, and know this. I'm going to pay you back—" She stopped at his amused glance. "*I am,*" she stated more slowly. "No matter what you think. Because I've changed. I care about that inn and I want to run that place without you."

Alex thought about her mother, and how much the inn had meant to her. He also knew how badly Susan had always sought her parents' approval—and had never gotten it. He said quite honestly, "I want that for you, too, Susan."

"I want you to stay away from Nicole."

"Jealous?"

She laughed, but he saw the quick spurt of heat in her eyes before they turned cool again, and he knew a moment of unease. "I mean it, Alex. Don't mess with me on this."

"And you're concerned because you care for her, is that it?" he asked, in an equally soft voice.

"I don't expect you to believe me, Alex. Nor will I bother to tell you I've changed my ways—you won't believe that either. Just steer clear of Nicole."

She left, shutting the door quietly. Alex let out a soft but vulgar expletive. He'd been convinced that Susan had lured Nicole up there for some self-serving purpose—which he now figured was money. Which was inadvertently *his* fault because he was the one Susan was trying to pay off.

God, he wanted to see Nicole. It'd been important that she make the first move, but he was tired of waiting. The path to the Wilson House was dark, but he didn't mind. The stars lit the way, and the wood-scented breeze felt good, so did the twigs and leaves crunching beneath his feet.

At the edge of the Wilson House property, he heard another set of footsteps. The slight figure walked toward him quickly, head down as if in heavy concentration, on a direct collision course with himself. He stopped and stood still.

"Hello, Nicole," he called softly, not wanting to startle her.

"Alex!" She jerked to a stop, putting her hand on her chest. "I didn't see you there."

They were a good hundred yards from the inn, hidden by the relative seclusion of the dark path. "This path isn't for night use," he said, not liking the idea of her walking alone. "You shouldn't be out here this late."

"I didn't think it would be a problem. I just wanted to walk. I bet this was a great place to grow up."

"It was." Slowly he drew her against him, ridiculously pleased she allowed it. Even more when she leaned into him. "Sometimes, like tonight," he said quietly, "I come out here just to feel a part of it."

"That's what I did tonight. And I pretend I belong here."

"You do."

She said nothing to that, just stood in his arms; chest to chest, thigh to thigh. Because he had to touch her, his hands slid over her back and up her sides, and he thought of when they'd made love beneath a beautiful night such as this one. It seemed like a dream now; soft, hazy, and perfect.

He wanted her again. Controlling his body's response to her was impossible.

In his arms, she froze, then with a choked sound, pulled back.

He sighed and shoved his hands in his pockets to keep them off her. "Nicole—"

"No," she said quickly, holding up a hand and taking another step back. "Don't say anything, you don't have to. It's my fault, I—"

"Wait," he said, grabbing her outstretched hand. "It's nobody's fault that I want you night and day, I just do."

"Night *and* day?"

"Yeah." With a little smile, he admitted, "And it's damn uncomfortable, let me tell you."

"Oh." Her eyes were wide. "It's different for me, I guess. I mean, I want you, too, but—" She slapped a hand over her mouth, looking horrified.

"There's nothing wrong with admitting that," he told her, laughing when she went red.

"It's *just* a physical ache," she corrected, poking him in the chest. "So don't get all cocky on me. Besides, it isn't me. I'm sure it would happen with anyone you hugged."

Just three minutes, he thought, just three minutes with each and every person who had ever stolen an ounce of her self-confidence. "Don't be so sure of that."

Now she looked worried. "But what if this . . . other thing wears off. Will you still want to be friends?"

"Forever."

"Isn't that difficult to know?" she asked skeptically. "I mean, how do you know you're still going to want to be friends with me in say, a year from now? Or even tomorrow?"

"I'm picky," he said. "But once I make a friend, it's for life."

She stared at him and he smiled. Good, he'd given her something to mull over for a while. It would be nice for her to have something positive to dwell on. He knew that to Nicole, the risks of being with him far outweighed any possible reward for her, even when those rewards went beyond her wildest imagination.

A breeze kicked up then, making the night cooler. The moon peeked out as the clouds shifted, and he watched with fascination as it lit the fiery highlights in her auburn hair. She caught him staring at her and gave him a little self-conscious smile. "What?"

"I think you're beautiful."

Her smile froze. "Well."

"I mean it," he told her. "You *are* beautiful, inside and out. Hasn't anyone ever told you that?"

She just looked at him, biting her lip.

"It doesn't matter," he said. "It's true." He saw the hesitation in her eyes, and he was reminded that something else, something much more than her feelings for him, was bothering her. "What is it?" he asked, but she only shook her head. "Maybe I can help."

"Maybe. I don't know. I have to think."

He had to accept that, though he didn't want to. "Just keep it in mind, then."

"I will. Good night," she whispered suddenly, running down the path. Not until she'd shut herself back in her room at the inn did she take a deep breath, and even then it took five minutes for her pulse to slow. His closeness certainly hadn't done a thing to relieve the claustrophobic feeling that had driven her to walk in the first place.

That man was dangerous to her heart. She could deny it from here until next year, but she was affected by him far more than just physically, and he knew it, damn him.

What was it about him? she wondered. What was it that made her ache so, when all her life she'd been able to avoid such a feeling. Why now? Why here, in the place she couldn't stay?

She plopped down on the large Victorian bed, her fingers closing around an envelope with a crinkling sound. Frowning, she brought it up. Inside, the note said: *Don't give up now.*

NINE

Nicole slept restlessly, Ted's file under her mattress causing an imaginary lump that she felt every time she moved. She dreamed of mysterious letters, of getting caught in Ted's office with her hands in his files, of having a real relationship with her family.

Last, she dreamed of warm, strong arms that held her close, murmuring soft words of love, and though she couldn't see his face, she knew that the voice and arms belonged to Alex.

Finally, at the first light of morning, she threw off the covers, giving up on sleep. In the kitchen, she found Candy leaning against the counter, sipping tea.

"Good morning," Candy said brightly. "I've come to offer my support here today. This will be the busiest day of the year because of the festival." Her smile faded as she studied Nicole. "Didn't you sleep well?"

She hadn't slept more than a wink since she'd read Ted's file and discovered Ella was not her mother. Now the note. She'd already dismissed both Brad and Susan from her mind, with the hunch the person who'd written it stood before her. "Is it that obvious?"

"No, not to someone who doesn't know you."

Nicole tilted her head, her gaze roaming over the older woman's features, the ones that so resembled her own that even now, weeks after having met Candy, it still startled her. "You don't know me," she replied, no insult intended.

"Oh, yes, I do." Candy calmly sipped her tea.

That rankled. "How's that? We've only spent a handful of minutes together."

"We're alike, you and I." Candy poured another cup of tea, then added lemon and sugar just the way Nicole liked it. She placed the cup in Nicole's hands, ignoring her look of surprise.

"The letter I got last night. It's from you."

Candy's brows drew together. "What letter?"

It was difficult not to scream her frustration, knowing that most likely Candy could answer her questions if she wanted to. "Right. Listen, I've got to leave."

"Are you going to the festival tonight? The inn and the resort are sharing a booth, and I'm manning this evening's shift. I thought maybe you'd come keep me company."

It touched her, dammit, even when she didn't want it to. "I'll be there."

Nicole prepared for the festival with misgivings. When Candy picked her up, they marveled at how many people seemed to fit into the small town. Krista sat in the booth, handing out brochures of the resort and inn.

"Hi, guys," she said. "Tourist season has arrived, and

I'm outta here." She stood and stretched. "At least until my next shift tomorrow night."

Candy laughed. "Alex suckered you, too, huh?"

Krista made a face. "Threatened to tell Mom and Dad if I didn't pull my weight. And believe me, he would."

"He knows how to get his way," Candy said, and Nicole couldn't agree more.

Krista left, and for the next hour Nicole and Candy talked to tourists, kids, locals, anyone who stopped by. After a while Nicole ventured away from the booth, curiously drawn to the rest of the festival that up until now she'd only heard, not seen.

The arts-and-crafts area, where many of the local artists had set up booths to display their wares, entertained her. Paintings of the surrounding landscape ingrained themselves in her mind, and she knew she'd never forget Sunrise Valley—no matter where she ended up.

She passed a makeshift stable, smiling politely when a young man called out to her to hop on the stagecoach. Looking around the crowd, Nicole couldn't help but notice everyone walked in pairs or groups, lovers and friends alike. All around her, people were having the time of their lives.

And though she hated the weakness of self-pity, she couldn't help it. Even surrounded by hundreds of people, Nicole had never felt more alone. She'd come to Sunrise Valley to learn about her past, and all she'd done was endanger her heart because of a man she'd have to leave when summer ended.

She found herself on a quiet street in front of a closed boutique, but something in the window caught her eye. The display looked like a picture from the past with a set of mannequins—man and wife, standing in front of their train station. Their little daughter sat on her suitcase, waiting for the train. It reminded her of the first picture she'd seen of her mother—or the person she'd thought was her mother. Her chest tightened.

She wouldn't cry, she thought desperately. Not now, not here. It wasn't such a difficult thing she wanted, other people everywhere took it for granted, every day of their lives. She simply wanted to know who she was and where she'd come from. It should have been so simple.

"Nicole."

She stiffened at the achingly familiar voice behind her, and she exhaled slowly without turning, struggling to regain her composure. How was it that he always found her when she felt so utterly vulnerable?

With gentle hands at her waist, he turned her to him. His deep eyes searched hers, seeing right through to her very wounded soul. "I've cried more since I've been here than I have in all my childhood years." She sniffed resentfully.

He wiped a tear from her cheek and searched his pockets, coming up with a wadded napkin. "I'd ask you what's wrong," he said in a rough-timbred voice that spoke of his concern. "But I doubt you'd tell me."

Surprisingly, one look into his strong, compelling eyes and she wanted to tell him everything. That was part of her problem. He might be used to such things, but she was not. Yet could she really regret the time he'd given her, the incredible feelings he'd taught her to feel?

Yes, dammit, especially when they hurt.

"I refuse to be sorry about that night," he said with a quietly defiant edge to his sexy voice.

"Stop reading my mind," she said gruffly, crossing her arms. "It's very unsettling."

"You're changing the subject," he chided gently. "I refuse to regret something that was the most incredible—"

"Don't!" she cried, mortified. He wasn't going to recall each and every detail, was he? Because then she'd want it again.

"No," he whispered angrily. "You don't. Don't do this to yourself, to us."

She whirled back to the window, escaping those knowing eyes, then caught her own reflection in the glass, hardly recognizing the pale, wide-eyed woman that blinked back at her.

"Are you afraid of me, Nicole?" His voice was quiet, defeated.

"No. Well, maybe a little," she admitted, watching his reflection in the window flinch, as though she'd struck him. "But only of what you make me feel. I used to be the envy of the other kids, you know. I wasn't afraid of anything. I'd squish a spider, hold a snake, go into a darkened room when no other kid would go. Nothing scared me. And yet now, standing here with you, I'm afraid."

His dark, intent gaze met hers in the window. "And I'm afraid of *not* being with you."

Too soon, too fast, she thought desperately, clinging to the wooden ledge. But God, she was helpless when he looked at her that way. "I'm not ready for this," she said urgently, panicky. "I don't want to hurt you." But she already had, she could see it in his eyes. "Look, for some people those things come naturally. They don't for me, I never learned how."

"It's *not* too late for you."

A little part of her wanted to believe that, desperately.

"Tell me, Nicole," he said, spinning her around, startling a gasp from her. "Tell me what you think is so wrong with you that we can't be together. Talk to me," he urged when she didn't respond, shaking her gently.

But she couldn't speak because the tenderness in his eyes was mixed with a hunger and a passion so great, it stole her breath. Then she saw fear there, too, and it humbled her to her socks. She wasn't even aware of the tears slipping unchecked down her cheeks until he slid the pad of his thumb over one. "Oh, baby, I'm sorry." He swore under his breath as he frantically searched for another napkin. "I had another . . ."

She glanced at the strong, tall man before her, so completely at ease with his own masculinity, he could admit to carrying spare napkins. The absurdity of it made her suddenly feel like giggling.

Alex went still, staring at her in surprise. "Are—" He bent, peering at her in the dark. "Are you by any chance, Ms. Sanders, *laughing* at me?"

She shook her head, but ruined it by letting another giggle escape.

"Now, that's a sound for sore ears," he said, grinning, opening his arms. "Come here."

Without hesitation, she walked into his hug, taking his offered strength and warmth, no longer wanting or willing to fight him. She lifted her head to tell him so. "Alex—" But the rest was muffled against his mouth.

He stole her breath, but still, she must have held something back because he made a soft sound of protest and whispered, "Let me in, Nicole. There's so much more than this."

As she wondered what he meant his mouth went on a

slow exploration of her face, touching everywhere her tears had fallen. Sighing with pleasure, she murmured, "This is enough for me. Please, let it be enough for you too."

"For now," he promised, dragging his lips over her neck. His teeth raked her earlobe and her knees wobbled. "For now." With relief that he wouldn't push, she let go of the last of her resistance, shivering in delight when his lips found hers again, and wound her arms tight around his neck as he pulled her closer. Time stopped as his possessive, hungry mouth took hers, proving how ridiculous she was for thinking she could keep her heart from him.

From somewhere, in a world far away, the sound of laughing voices moved closer as another couple passed by them on the street. Nicole jerked back, embarrassed to have gotten caught necking on the street like a teenager.

Alex smiled smugly, resting his hands on her waist. "Don't worry. That's just a physical reaction. It'll fade in a moment."

She narrowed her eyes to retort when she caught the sound of his ragged breathing. "You're affected too."

Laughing softly, he rested his forehead against hers. "I never claimed different." After a minute, when his breathing evened out, he whispered, "I'd never hurt you, Nicole."

She looked at his endearing, familiar face. "I know."

"So tell me why you were crying."

"I—okay."

His smile was slow and warm and made her heart catch. He slipped an arm around her. "I know just the place."

He took her to the rock on the lake, where they sat

listening to the wind blow through the trees, the water lapping softly against the sand. Watching the moon cast a white shimmering light on the lake, Nicole felt the first peace she'd felt in a long time.

Alex didn't rush her, and if he was impatient, he gave no sign of it. They sat in companionable silence, absorbing the beauty of the night. Finally, Nicole glanced at him and saw the unfamiliar lines of fatigue and worry on his face. Had she done that to him?

She spoke in the chilly air, the sudden sound of her voice startling even herself. "I'm sorry, Alex. I'm really not very good at this one-night-stand thing." She stared at the water, feeling unsophisticated and far out of her league.

His soft smile vanished. "Nicole, what we did was much more than a one-night stand, it's just that you've refused to nurture it since then." He shifted closer, until their thighs touched. "It started here." He patted the rock beneath them. "When I first saw you, I knew you were someone I wanted to meet. But then the attraction grew." Taking her hand, he brought it to his chest, rubbing it against the spot where his heart beat out steady and strong. "It ended up here," he whispered, "until I could think of little else but you." He brought her hand to his lips and kissed her fingers. "So that night when you showed up on my deck, looking as lonely as I felt, it just seemed right. It still seems right."

"But—"

"I know," he said grimly, taking a deep breath. "I made you a promise that this was enough, and I meant it. I won't be pushing you, Nicole, into something you're not ready for."

She'd been so sure a minute earlier, damn him, that she could walk away anytime. Now she wasn't sure of anything, except she wanted to weep, wanted desperately for him to hold her again. Confused, she made to stand, but he stopped her, his eyes probing deep, his voice soft and calm. "Are you pregnant, Nicole?"

He showed no panic, no fear at the prospect of her carrying his child. He had to be the strongest man she'd ever met—certainly strong enough to shoulder vast amounts of responsibility, but thankfully, this time it wasn't required. "No. It isn't that."

"Are you sure?"

"Yes," she mumbled, baffled by the easy acceptance and soft tenderness in his eyes.

"All right," he said, sounding almost disappointed. "So what is it?"

She reached into her shorts pockets, past the smooth pebble she still kept there, and pulled out the envelope she'd found on her bed. "There's this for starters. I also found Ella's records, and discovered she was in a car accident when she was young. There were . . . major complications."

Watching her intently, he frowned. "Such as?"

"She couldn't have children, Alex."

Thoughtfully, calmly, he rubbed his chin. "So Ella's not your mother. That makes sense."

Nicole shouldn't have been amazed at how he simply took her word without question. Was this what it would be like to be with him? This easy? Standing abruptly, she walked toward the water, her arms wrapped around herself.

"What does your birth certificate say?" he asked, coming up behind her.

"Can you believe that I've never seen it?" She shook her head with a self-mocking smile. In tenth grade she'd wanted to go to Europe with her French class, but Maddie had refused to help her fund the trip. So she hadn't gone—and hadn't gotten a passport. If only she had, she would have seen her birth certificate long before. "I tried to get a copy from the recorder's office. I was adopted at birth and my records are sealed."

His big hands settled on her shoulders. "I'm sorry."

Because it was easier to stand alone, she stepped away from him, from his comfort, and everything else he offered. "I've petitioned the state to open my records."

"No wonder you've been distracted."

"Yeah, and full of self-pity."

"Oh, I'd say you're entitled," he said lightly. "How did you get ahold of Ella's records?"

To test him, and maybe herself, she turned back to face him. "I stole them from Ted's office." Now, she thought. Now he'd turn from her. Desert her.

His face went slack with disbelief. "You . . . stole them."

He was horrified. She'd asked for it, hadn't she? Her life would be lonely without him in it, but she couldn't resist defending herself. "I knew Ted was lying about something, so I went to see him. I had to wait in his office and the files were there."

"They weren't locked?"

"Well," she said slowly, avoiding his gaze. "The keys were on his desk."

He stared at her for what seemed like forever, and she shifted uncomfortably, wishing he'd get it over with. Tell her how sorry he was, but that he couldn't be with someone like her. And she'd go on her way. Miserably.

Then, suddenly, he grinned. "Tell me, Sherlock Holmes," he said, the grin splitting his face from ear to ear. "Were you discovered?"

"Of course not," she said indignantly, then ruined it by grinning back.

"You're amazing."

"I had to do it, Alex. He lied to me. I belong to one of them, and I just want the truth. Is that asking so much?"

"No, of course not."

She wished he'd touch her, but she knew he would never do that again. Not now. Now when he knew exactly how low she'd sink to get what she wanted. The wind kicked up, stirring her hair, causing goose bumps on her bare legs. "Neither Ted nor Candy wanted to claim me. They're embarrassed—"

"Stop it."

Her head snapped up at the harsh tone she'd never heard from him before. "Why?" she asked bitterly. "It's the truth. Why else would they hide it?"

"I don't know," he said tersely, "but that's not what I meant." Moving so fast she didn't even have time to step back, he grabbed her shoulders. "Stop expecting me to take off, Nicole." Hauling her against him, he unbalanced her world with a sudden gentleness she couldn't bear. "I'm not going anywhere, I promise you, so stop testing me. I don't care that you broke into Ted's files, I would have done the same thing. Hell, I would have done it for you if you'd let me," he said against her hair, rocking her. "God, Nicole, let me in. Please, let me in your life."

"I'm trying," she whispered. "It's hard."

"I know." He hugged her tight, then let her go. "But at least demand an explanation—you just might get it."

"I want to wait for my birth certificate."

His brow creased. "Bull. You're avoiding the confrontation."

"Ridiculous."

"Is it?" he asked with a sad, small smile. "I don't think so. You're adopted and you want to know why. *Ask them.*"

Ask them. It should have been easy. But it wasn't, and she couldn't. In quiet despair, she turned from him and stared sightlessly at the lake. She heard his quiet oath, knew it was caused by frustration.

"You don't want to know. It's that simple."

Resentment flared, clawing its way past her heart. "And what would you know of this? You've had family around you your entire life. Your cabin is filled with pictures of people who know and love you. You have a thousand happy memories. I have none of those things."

His arms wrapped around her, wouldn't retreat even when she squirmed in protest and anger. "You could start from this point," he said in a low voice, restraining her as he spoke earnestly. "You could live your life exactly as you want to, bringing new people you care about into your life. People who care about you."

Surrounded by him, she had no choice but to listen to his words. Through her clothes she could feel the steady beat of his heart, the roughness of his jeans against the back of her thighs, and she sought that mindless passion she knew he could give her. Closer, she thought, shifting to fit herself better against him. His arms tightened as he touched her with terrifying tenderness.

"I made you a promise, Nicole," he whispered huskily. "I promised I wouldn't push for what you couldn't give, and I meant it. Be damn sure about this next move."

Unable to help herself, she shifted again, wringing a low moan from him. Under the hem of her sweater his hands slipped, spreading wide over her middle, stopping just short of her aching breasts. She sucked her breath in sharply.

"Nicole?"

God, she had to shake her head to see straight, and to remember, this wasn't simply lust, this was something much deeper, much scarier. But he was waiting for a decision she wasn't ready to make.

He'd stiffened when she didn't answer, and she didn't blame him.

Retrieving his hands, he backed away from her. "You're chasing demons again," he said flatly, and her heart stopped at the hurt in his voice.

"I'm sorry," she whispered. "I just can't."

"Then I can't either."

Unexpectedly, her eyes filled, and he made a wordless sound of remorse before pulling her back for an embrace meant to soothe, not excite. He sighed. "It's all right, Nicole. It's going to be all right."

Burrowing into his shoulder, she held on tight. "I'm sorry, don't give up on me. Not yet."

His grip tightened. "Not a chance."

TEN

Alex left her alone for a week, and by the end of that time, Nicole had drummed up a thousand silly little excuses to go to the resort to see him. She ignored them all, but fretted that she'd finally pushed him away for good.

She didn't want that, and the more time that passed, the more she was sure of it. The only problem was she had no idea what she did want.

Finally one early morning she slipped out the back door of the inn, after having helped herself to a small bag of Susan's fresh muffins. The air felt chilly, even for summer, but after a few minutes of brisk walking up the path, she had her sweatshirt tied around the waist of her shorts.

She hesitated at the lodge, nervous. Was it too early? Would he be sleeping? What would she say? With a small sigh, she headed toward his cabin, unable to help remembering the last time she'd been there. *On his patio, in his arms.* A little heat stole into her just thinking about it.

From the driveway, she could hear banging. It came from the shed off the side of the house.

She was right outside the door when the noise abruptly stopped. An imaginative and exceptionally vulgar curse rent the morning air, making her eyes widen in surprise. Biting back her laughter, she walked to the opening, curious.

A Waverunner sat on a rack in the center of the large shed, but what caught Nicole's immediate attention was the pair of long, lean legs, firmly encased in a pair of jeans so worn, they were nearly white. The rest of Alex was deeply buried in the engine cavity, but she could hear him muttering to himself.

She smiled, appreciating the view, but that smile faded quickly. What kind of reception would she receive? She knocked softly on the side of the shed. "Alex?"

He jerked upright, bumping his head. Swearing and holding his forehead, he disentangled himself and slowly straightened. His expression, when he saw her, was comical.

"Sorry to startle you," she said, unable to contain her grin.

Frowning, he rubbed his head. "How long have you been there?"

"Long enough to learn some new words."

His face reddened. "Great."

His dark hair stuck straight up in places, matted down in others. The smudge of grease across his T-shirt covered his bare arm, too, and the knees of his jeans were completely gone. She could smell soap and warm skin, and thought he looked rumpled, rugged, and one-hundred-percent rough and tough male.

The bottom line was—she wanted him.

The quick flash of pleasure that crossed his face relieved her, but it was short-lived. He recovered quickly, looking at her with a carefully blank expression. "You've been avoiding me."

"No, I've been busy." The lie choked her. "All right, maybe I have. But . . ." She took a big breath. "I missed you. Dammit."

He grinned. "Did you now?"

"Yeah. But don't ask me to repeat it." She held up the small bag of muffins she'd sneaked. "I even brought a peace offering, in case I needed it."

The hesitation in her eyes killed him, so did the thought of her thinking she needed to coax him into wanting to be with her. "Forget the muffins. Come here and kiss me."

She let out a nervous little laugh. "That wouldn't be wise." But she stepped into the shed. "I'm sorry if I hurt you, Alex. I never wanted to do that."

"Don't apologize for your feelings, Nicole. Don't ever apologize for them. I wouldn't have left you alone much longer, it's just that you seemed to need some peace." He wiped his hands on a cloth, tossed it aside, using the distraction to look away because the sight of her standing there in the morning light made him want to drag her down to the cold cement floor and bury himself deep inside her.

"What is that?"

For a minute he thought she meant his huge erection. But her eyes were on the watercraft, and he felt incredibly stupid. "A Waverunner. Ever been on one?"

She paused. "No."

The answer was simple enough, but he'd seen a worldful of answers in those eyes of hers. She'd probably never been given the chance to do something as frivolous as frolic lakeside. She'd been too busy trying to survive. "Want to try it once?"

Her eyes shifted to the long, sleek body of the small craft. "I don't think so."

"Chicken?"

Her gaze snapped up, meeting his. There was humor there, as he'd hoped. "When I was a kid," she said, "I'd never turn down a dare."

He'd counted on it. "And now?" He could picture her as a rough, dark-haired, petite beauty, taking on the world.

"I'm smarter now. I hope." She looked at the Waverunner warily.

"Come on, we'll make a day of it. I'll even pack the picnic." He smiled enticingly, wondering what he thought he was doing. The woman didn't trust him, and he was doing what he'd promised he wouldn't—practically begging. Oh . . . what the hell. "Please?"

His heart did a slow roll in his chest when she turned and looked at him. It was there, he thought wildly, his pulse taking off at the emotions shining from her eyes, she just didn't know it yet. Tugging her closer, he cupped her face, drinking in the sight of her looking at him.

"You know I can't think when you do that."

"No?" he murmured, stroking her jaw with his thumb.

She backed up, her breath unsteady. "No, definitely can't think when you do that. Promise I won't drown?"

"What?"

"On that thing." She gestured to the Waverunner.

He smiled, having no idea how his next words were going to haunt him. "I promise," he said confidently. "Next weekend, then?"

She nodded. "I have to go."

"I know." He brushed a stray strand of hair from her face, liking the way it felt between his fingers. The heavy waves fell past her shoulders, and the morning sun lit it up like fire. "It's beautiful," he said softly, watching her eyes fill with confusion and desire at his touch. She breathed as if she'd run a mile. Uphill. Biting back the smug smile tugging at his lips, he leaned in a little, knowing he was going to kiss her. The pulse at the base of her throat grew frenzied.

"I really have to go." But she didn't move. "I'm needed at the inn, it's a full house." When he still just stared at her without a word, she asked, "What?"

He had to taste her, *really* taste her. He pulled her between his thighs, wrapped her face in his hands, and touched his lips to hers. She was everything he remembered, but then she opened her mouth for him and he couldn't remember anything at all. He kissed her until she made that soft, helpless sound in her throat, until he knew she was as breathless as he. Slowly, he lifted his head, pulled back his hands, and whispered, "You have to go."

She stood still a minute, her eyes misty with bafflement and arousal. When they cleared, she took a careful step backward and slid her hands into her pockets. "Well."

He grinned. He'd seen those slim hands shake before she'd slipped them away. She still wasn't ready to accept him. But he was a patient man, he reminded himself. Real patient, especially when there was something worth waiting for. He thought Nicole Sanders just might be worth the wait.

He watched as, without a word, she turned and ran

down his driveway to the path that would lead her back to the inn.

"That looked serious."

Alex turned to see Krista standing on the gravel drive, wearing a curious smile. "Tell me that's coffee," he said greedily, looking at the tall thermos in her hand.

She stepped closer, poured him a cup. "Lori and Robin sent me."

He didn't pause until he had given himself a good healthy dose of caffeine, and a moment to settle his pumping heart.

His younger twin sisters were both married, each with two kids. They both lived in Redlands on the same street and spent each and every spare moment together, comparing visions, as they called them. Their greatest trial in life was that neither Krista nor Alex had expanded their family.

"Let me guess," he said. "They found someone for me."

Krista smiled as she repoured, then took the cup for herself. "No." She sipped calmly, studying him over the rim. "They said you've done that for yourself."

Alex stared, then laughed uneasily. "They're amazing."

"Are they right?"

He shrugged. "Maybe." He thought of how Nicole had looked after that last kiss. Stunned . . . and sexy as hell. Oh, he wanted her again, more than he could have thought possible, but it was much more than the physical yearning he felt now. He wanted her mind and her heart as well. "Yeah, they're right."

She reached for his hand, her face serious. "You don't look as happy as I'd expect. Don't tell me she's resisting, not after that kiss I just witnessed."

Again, he smiled uneasily. He'd never get used to his sisters butting their way into his life, gleaning details, making up what they didn't know until they had the whole picture. But what they did, they did out of a fierce, protective love, a love he never took for granted. And he returned that love, a hundredfold. "You could say she's not as sure as I am."

"Oh, Alex," she said softly, hugging him close. "How could she not know? What's the matter with that girl?" She pulled back. "I'll talk to her."

"No!" He took his sister's shoulders to hold her back from rushing to battle for him. "Krista, please. She's . . . not had an easy time. She didn't grow up the way we did, with lots of wild, crazy siblings who put their noses into everyone else's business. You'd scare her off."

"Didn't she have a grandmother or someone?"

"She had no one but herself." And that was the crux of it, he thought. She'd never had anyone to depend on, or at least no one who had hung around long enough to give her a sense of security. As a result, she'd created a comfort zone around her that she allowed no one to penetrate. As long as she didn't allow anyone to get too close, they couldn't hurt her. "But she's got me now."

"Alex, I hate to bring this up, but she's related to Susan." Krista's nose wrinkled in distaste. "You know, the woman who made your life a living hell for—"

"She's not like Susan."

"Yeah, but does she *know* about Susan?" Krista asked pointedly, recapping her coffee. "No? Don't you think that's a bad idea? You should tell her, Alex, or rest assured, Susan will. And you can bet her version won't look good for you."

Nicole found Susan in the kitchen, folding towels. Worried about what she had to do, Nicole smiled, but Susan saw right past it.

"What's wrong?"

Nicole lifted her hands, full of receipts and check registers, and tried to not feel sick. "We're short money. Again."

Susan's color faded.

"Susan? What is it?"

Her cousin sat down heavily and wearily covered her face. "It's Brad." Nicole's stomach twisted. "Every time he checks someone out, he claims there's problems and he gives a refund. I used to believe him, but I can't anymore."

Nicole stared at her. "He's pocketing money and you let it continue? Susan, you're one of the smartest, most competent businesswomen I know. *What's the matter with you?*"

"He's my brother."

Those simple, but heartfelt words had Nicole sinking into the closest chair. What she knew about loyalty to family would fit in her back pocket. Who was she to condemn Susan?

"That's why I got so far behind in my payments to Alex," Susan said quietly, wringing the towel with her hands. "I pay back everything Brad takes, but it comes out of my own pocket and I don't have much."

"Oh, Susan."

Susan dropped her hands and her head came up proudly. "I'd do anything for him, Nicole. He's my family."

"You can't keep protecting him," Nicole said gently. "He needs help. He's gambling, then?"

"I think so. He spends all his spare time in Reno or on the lake with his friends in that speedboat."

"Does Alex know?"

Susan jumped to her feet. "God, no. And he can't. He'll have Brad arrested for sure. I've put it all back except for five hundred. And I'll get that back soon, I promise." She took Nicole's hands and knelt at her feet. "Please, Nicole, you can't tell him. He'd *never* understand."

"He would," Nicole insisted, praying it was true.

"No," Susan said, panicked. "You don't understand. Please, promise you won't tell him."

Something in Susan's wild look had Nicole shifting uneasily. "You're putting me in a tough position, Susan. Asking me not to tell my boss about a problem with his own money."

Susan's eyes turned cold and she stood with dignity. "My mistake," she said quietly. "I thought you'd choose to help me over him."

"Susan—"

"It's okay, you don't owe me anything, and you don't understand about Alex. You couldn't."

"I would if you'd tell me."

"He's a coldhearted man, Nicole," Susan said, folding her hands. "I'm not going to go into details about it, that would be gossiping, and since he's not here to defend himself, it would also be unfair. All I'm asking is that you give me some time before you tell him what you need to. Brad is better, I'm helping him, and he'll be fine."

She wanted no part in deceiving Alex. "How much time?"

Susan smiled in relief, impulsively hugging Nicole. "I knew you'd help me."

"How much time, Susan?"

"A month," Susan said. "If things haven't changed by then, I'll convince Brad to get professional help, I swear."

By the end of the week, Nicole was missing another five hundred dollars.

Nicole looked at the calendar one late summer day, surprised to see that in four weeks she'd have to go back to San Francisco and her teaching job.

Alex had come by every day, alternately gentle and unabashedly flirtatious. He had her in a state of such swirling, uneven emotions, she could hardly think, much less work, and she suspected he knew that—and enjoyed it.

But she felt overwhelmed with guilt.

She hadn't told him about the missing money from the Wilson House account. Every day she approached Susan, begging her to tell Alex—or let Nicole tell him—and every day Susan paid back the money out of her own pocket so Nicole wouldn't feel bad.

Friday afternoon Nicole sat alone in the office, the late, hot sun pouring through the open window. The enormity of what she'd done made her groan and drop her face into her hands, agonizing. She'd betrayed Alex.

For the first time in her life she gave considerable thought to breaking a promise. But would Susan forgive her? Would Alex? Nicole knew enough about him to know he'd consider this a great breach of their trust in each other.

Brad made the mistake of happening by her door at that moment.

"Brad!" She bit down on her own temper when she saw how pleased he looked with himself.

"Hey, cuz." He smiled broadly. "Miss me?"

"Do well this week, Brad? Win big?"

His smile faded somewhat. "What?"

"I know you were gambling. What I don't know is if you won."

"Yeah," he said, slipping his hands in his pockets and rocking back on his heels. He couldn't keep the pride from his voice. "I won."

"Good." Nicole smiled, lifting a palm. "Then pay up, buddy. You owe the account."

"Nicole, what are you doing?" Susan stood in the doorway, wringing her hands.

"Something you should have done a long time ago," Nicole said, her eyes on Brad. "There's more money missing, Susan. You can't keep covering for him, it isn't fair to you—or him. Either we do this now, or I have to call Alex."

Brother and sister made little nervous sounds, and Nicole forced her heart to harden. "This is the right thing," she said, more to convince herself. But it was hard to see the twin looks of disappointment, directed at her.

Brad pulled some money from his pocket. "I don't have the whole thing."

"I thought you said you won."

"I had . . . expenses," he said with a little glance at his sister.

Nicole could imagine the loan sharks hovering over him, waiting to break a kneecap or worse. "Oh, Brad," she said sadly. "You've got to stop. For no other reason than it's wrong."

"It isn't all his fault," Susan began. "I let him do it."

"And you've got to stop blaming yourself," Nicole said, turning to her. She took her cousin's cold hands in hers. "You can't be his mother and father, Susan. You just can't." Susan's eyes filled, breaking Nicole's heart—because she understood. "You can only be his sister. Together, you and I, we can be his friend too. And make sure he gets the help he needs."

Susan sniffed indelicately, and Nicole had to smile at the first spontaneous thing she'd ever seen her cousin do. "This used to be our mom's place," Susan said quietly. "It was smaller then, but still successful. There was always cash. She let us have some whenever we needed. Then she died . . . and it was ours. Well," she said with a little sigh directed at her brother, "mine really, since I was the one who worked, but I still let Brad have money whenever he needed. Just like Mom. Even after Alex became involved, I continued it. We never talked about it, and to tell you the truth, I never considered it stealing because I still think of the inn as mine."

Nicole could understand how it happened, but it didn't make it right. "But—"

"I know," Susan said, her voice harsh. "It isn't fair to Alex. Well, I don't really care about being fair to Alex, for reasons you can't possibly understand. But I do care about doing something illegal, so I decided you were right. I started putting the money back that Brad took." She looked at Brad apprehensively. "I just hadn't told him that yet."

"Sus," Brad said in surprised regret. "I'm sorry."

Nicole rolled her eyes. "Jeez, you guys! Do you ever

communicate? All these years I've wanted family around me, but what for? Nobody talks. Nobody listens."

Brad laughed, more in relief than anything else. "Welcome to family life. We like each other only because we have to."

"Brad! It's more than that," Susan said, slapping his arm, laughing back. "Tell her."

"Oh, all right," he said, sighing. "Not only do we *have* to like each other, we have to have dinner together at least once a week and pretend to be interested in each other's lives."

Susan rolled her eyes, looking disgusted. But she was smiling, and Nicole caught on. They loved each other, despite their differences, their faults. No matter what happened, that would never change. The pang of jealousy Nicole experienced both surprised and hurt.

"I promise to be good from here on out," Brad said cajolingly. "Really, this time. You believe me, don't you?"

Nicole was sure that smile of his had gotten him just about anything he wanted in the past, but she couldn't resist smiling back. "I have no doubt you'll try."

"It's all settled, then. Let's make up." He kissed each of them soundly. "Love you," he claimed, "but gotta go."

He disappeared out of the door before Nicole could remind him he hadn't actually given her a cent. Susan sighed. "I'll get it to you. For the last time," she promised as Nicole opened her mouth. "And I swear to you, it won't happen again. Just, please, *don't tell Alex.*"

Nicole hesitated, knowing Brad needed help.

"If it happens again," Susan promised, "I'll tell Alex myself, okay?"

"How come you never ask your father for help?"

Susan's lips thinned. "He believes his children are hopeless and irresponsible, I didn't see any reason to confirm it."

It wasn't until much later, when Nicole sat alone on the veranda sipping tea, that the anger for Ted really kicked in. What kind of a father ignored his children simply because they hadn't turned out as he'd expected or wanted?

Was *she* Ted's child? Had he turned his back on her as well?

She looked around her at the calm, serene beauty of the mountains. No matter what she discovered, by summer's end she'd be back in the city. She'd miss it here.

Alex. She'd miss him the most. Those laughing eyes. His easy companionship. How he looked at her as if she were the only woman on earth.

As if she'd summoned him, he strode onto the porch, a tool belt slung low on his hips, all that easy long-legged grace moving toward her. When he saw her a slow smile curved his lips.

"I came to see a broken lock," he said. "But seeing you is much better."

ELEVEN

Nervously, she jumped to her feet. She had no right fantasizing about the man she'd lied to. None at all. In fact, she should just tell him, tell him right here and now what she'd done so she could get on with her life.

"Don't take off on my account," Alex said, his smile gone, his voice quiet.

"I wasn't. I—"

Stepping closer, his warm, appraising eyes met hers, and whatever she was going to say flitted out of her head. So did any rational thoughts. Needing something to do with her hands, she fumbled with her sweater. Alex took it from her shaking fingers and stepped behind her to help her slip into it, his hands gliding over her shoulders for far longer than necessary. Her heart gave a funny, traitorous lurch.

"I can't stop thinking about you," he murmured in her ear, "I've tried, but I can't."

Of their own accord, her eyes closed. Didn't she have the same problem? His wonderful body heat seeped into her back and thighs, and it was everything she could do not to strain against him. When she trembled slightly with the effort, she attributed it to a chill.

He knew different, judging by the little knowing sound that came from his throat. "Miss me?"

"No." But her voice was a mere whisper, her breath too quick.

"Liar." He laughed softly, sexily, running a finger down her neck.

God, the man could turn her on without trying, and that knowledge had her gritting her teeth. Until he replaced his fingers with his lips, making her pulse hammer. Feeling bewildered, a little light-headed, and very inexperienced, she stepped from him with great effort and buttoned her sweater. "You're busy."

"I'd rather stay and talk to you."

Given the hooded look his eyes had taken on, she doubted he had talking in mind. "I don't think so."

He took a step toward her and she found herself hedged between the railing and his tall, very solid form. With a hand on either side of her, he softly trailed his lips from her ear to her cheek. "Then let's kiss," he suggested. Her stomach somersaulted wildly. He touched his lips to the corner of her mouth, keeping his eyes wide open on hers. "You want to."

She turned her head at the last minute, and his whispery kiss landed on her cheek harmlessly. Unruffled, he kissed each eye softly. "I want you, Nicole. You want me back. I dream of you telling me." His hands settled on her hips, squeezing gently.

"You promised not to push me." Was that breathless voice hers?

Lifting his hands palms up, he raised his eyebrows, and Nicole realized with horror that it was *her* leaning on *him*, *her* gripping *his* shoulders. The look he sent her was innocent, harmless. As if he could ever be that, she thought, backing away. Dangerous to her heart and soul, but never, ever harmless.

"You don't have to touch me to be pushing," she said ungraciously, crossing her arms. "You only have to look at me."

Laughing, he pulled her close again. "Know what I think?"

"Don't think I can repeat it." But she let herself relax against him, surprised at how perfectly her head fit into the curve of his shoulder.

He laughed again and held her tight. "God, you're good for me. I think I'm good for you too. Kiss me, Nicole."

The huskiness of his voice, combined with his incredible ability to melt her to his whim, was nearly her undoing. In horror, she realized she was a breath away from giving in completely, to doing exactly as he suggested. "You can't always have what you want." But she didn't back away, couldn't, not when he felt so good.

"I know that."

"What is it about you?" she asked in genuine bewilderment. "What is it that makes me tell you things I don't mean to, do things with you that . . . that I've never done before?"

Eyes sparkling with dangerous humor, he opened his mouth, but before he could say anything, she said, exasperated, "If you laugh at me, I'll have to hurt you."

"I'm not laughing at you." But he was smiling that wide confident smile that made her want to punch him. "It's called trust, Nicole. Trust is what makes you want to tell me things, do things that you've never done before." He waited a minute while she soaked that in. "Do you like it?"

"No!" She crossed her arms over her middle, rocking herself in an unconscious gesture from her childhood. "No, I don't. Not at all."

"Maybe it'll grow on you."

"I doubt it," she said with dismay, thinking that if she really trusted him, she would have told him sooner about the missing money—no matter what she'd promised Susan.

"Someday, Nicole," he said with hope tingeing that smile. "Someday you'll trust me." Even in the dwindling daylight, she had no problem reading the yearning, the hunger in his eyes. His voice was thick, rough, and edgy. "With your heart."

He meant it, she could see it in his shattering intensity, his utter stillness as he waited for her response. Her throat tightened. "So much for not pushing," she said, striving for a light tone.

His mouth tightened. "I'm sorry. You're right." Backing away from her, he moved across the veranda. "I'll be around, Nicole. If you need me."

Then he left her alone.

Saturday dawned with spectacular potential. By the time Alex picked Nicole up in the Blazer, towing the Waverunner, the sun burned warm and lazy and the sky flowed with fluffy, cotton clouds.

It should have been perfect, but Nicole couldn't help but feel on edge as they drove the short distance to the landing dock at the lake. Why had she promised to spend an entire day with him? She couldn't possibly resist him that long, couldn't possibly relax with the lie between them.

She hated liars, and at that moment she hated herself.

Just tell him. But she could see the joy on his face at the prospect of a day off, of a day with her. She could see the ice chest and picnic basket he'd prepared in the backseat, so she swallowed the thoughts, where they stuck like a ball of lead in her throat.

They found a secluded beach. Nicole sat at the water's edge, listened to the birds chatter. Alex stretched his long legs beside her. "I think this is my first day off this year."

She looked at him, saw the tense lines of stress around his mouth, and her guilt doubled. "Krista told me about the problems with the day-care. What's going to happen?"

"I don't know." He rolled his shoulders as if trying to ease the strain. He glanced at her, saw her worry. "It'll be all right."

Her heart twisted, knowing he deserved better from her. "Is it finished?"

"Not yet. Just got my last shipment of materials, though. Should have it done in no time." He looked away, jaw tight.

"Alex," she said, her chest feeling too heavy. "I'm supposed to be your friend." That was a joke, she thought bitterly. She'd done nothing to deserve the title.

"You are."

She shook her head. "If I was, you'd lean on me the way you let me lean on you."

His eyes met hers, deep and probing. "All right, then. Someone's trying to block the expansion."

"Who?"

"I'm not sure yet."

"I'm sorry, Alex."

"I have my materials, finally. It should be all right now." He took her hand. "Find out who sent you that letter yet?"

"No." At his look, knowing he was about to push, she said, "Alex, let's not argue today."

"You mean, we should agree to disagree on the matter and forget it for now?"

"Something like that."

Standing, he pulled her up. "Well, if you don't want to argue, you won't want the alternative either, so let's go out on the water." He pulled off his shirt, exposing the most magnificent chest she'd ever seen.

She couldn't take her eyes off him, and judging by the little smile he gave her, he knew it. "Something wrong?"

"Of course not." But she had to clear her throat. She pulled off her sweatshirt and shorts, self-consciously straightening her swimsuit. Feeling horribly exposed, she hurriedly yanked on the wet suit Alex had brought her. Moving behind her, Alex whispered, "Let me." And he zipped it slowly up, the metal-on-metal sound making her shiver. Or maybe it was just feeling his breath on her neck and picturing his hands on her back. Disgusted with herself and her strange inability to control her libido around him, she put on a life vest, then waded out behind him, watching him push the Waverunner.

"What if we fall off the thing and it keeps going?" she asked apprehensively. The watercraft seemed so huge in the water.

"Then it idles and moves in a wide circle. We just swim to it. It's easier than it sounds."

Hopping on, he started it, then pulled her up behind him. Nervous and unsure, Nicole glanced down at the choppy water. The engine seemed loud, and she couldn't figure out where to put her hands.

He leaned back and turned his head, speaking near her ear over the noise. "I'll go real easy, okay? Just tell me if I'm doing something you don't like, and we'll stop."

She swallowed hard at the images his soft-spoken words provoked. On top of that, with her legs spread around the outside of his, her chest plastered to his back, she had no choice but to think erotic thoughts. But as they passed the buoys designating the five-mile-per-hour zone and Alex hit the gas, all thoughts flew from her head except survival. Biting back her scream, she gripped him tight, eyes shut.

Less than a minute later she realized something. It felt incredibly exciting to have the wind ripping through her hair, to feel the sting of the fresh water on her face. Cautiously, she opened her eyes, and laughed with delight at the quickly passing shoreline.

Alex increased their speed. When they reached a jut of land and had to turn, she clutched at him, thinking that they couldn't make the tight turn without spilling off. Still, he didn't slow. Ducking her head down behind his broad shoulders, she held her breath, waiting.

His chest vibrated with what felt like a laugh, then he slowed. "You okay?"

She realized she held him incredibly close to her, her fingers digging into his hips. Raising her head, she smiled sheepishly. "Yeah."

"Want to drive?" He killed the engine and they bobbed on the water, surrounded by a sudden hush except for the slap of the water against the Waverunner.

Nicole looked at what was little more than a motorcycle on a deck and shook her head. "There's no room for me to get off and get in front. We'll tip."

"No problem." Before she could utter another excuse, he dove neatly off, surfacing a second later with a broad grin. Effortlessly, he pulled himself up behind her. "Done."

She gasped when his long, wet arms wrapped around her. Then he moved snug against her back, his legs pressing against the outside of hers.

"Afraid?"

"No," she said, wriggling. "You're freezing!"

He laughed softly and pulled her closer. "Keep wriggling like that and cold isn't the only thing you'll be."

She froze, vibrantly aware of the juncture of his thighs nestled to her bottom. That they were still separated by two thick life jackets didn't matter in the least—having him molded to her was . . . startling. Her heart raced.

"What do I do?" she managed to ask.

Putting his hands over hers, he directed them on the controls. "Here's the gas. Once you get up to speed, the steering is much more responsive." She didn't think it possible, but once she got started, she really was okay. The sense of power, being in control . . . She loved it. Laughing with pleasure, she increased the speed, and actually forgot she wasn't alone until Alex reached around her and took over, slowing them down.

There was another boat, the first they'd seen. The driver held up a red flag, and there was a skier in the water. Alex steered them clear. "Boats don't like these things much," he said. "Especially when there's a skier in the water. It's safest to keep away."

They played for another hour before returning to

shore. Nicole grabbed a drink and plopped down on her towel, surprised at how tired she was.

Alex remained standing, removing his vest. Tossing it to a towel, he peeled off his clinging wet suit, leaving just his swimming trunks.

"Isn't it an incredible feeling?" he asked, his eyes still on the water.

The incredible feeling came from watching him, with what precious little he wore clinging to his dripping wet, built body. "Yes," she managed, her throat suddenly dry.

"It can be any season," he continued, "and when I'm here, my problems drift away." He turned to her then, his eyes shining with affection and a neediness that stole her breath. Before she could say anything, he came to her, dropping to his knees to unclip her life jacket. "You have to remove this and the wet suit so they'll dry." He slid it off her shoulders and reached around her to unzip the wet suit. "We'll put them in the sun so they'll be warm when you want them again."

Nicole stood up and peeled herself out of the wet suit, praying her swimsuit stayed in one place. Her body tingled from his gaze, the air sizzled with a hot sexual tension. Nicole held her breath against it. She had no business doing this. Being attracted to a man was one thing, she could handle that. But this desperate longing for something she couldn't name scared her, and scared her deep.

Tell him, she told herself. Tell him about the money now. But she knew if she did, he'd think she'd gone along with him on this trip to soften him so he wouldn't be so furious with her and her cousins. Cornered in her own trap, she stood there, wringing her hands.

Alex still knelt on her towel at her feet, watching her with a quiet look. "Nicole. Not again."

"What?"

"You're standing right there in front of me, and you just withdrew into a shell. You're a thousand miles away." He stood, biting back his frustrated sigh when she denied it with a small shrug. When he took her shoulders in his hands, she stiffened, but he didn't let go. It was time, he thought, time for her to start to trust him. "Nicole. You're faking that smile right now."

She glared at him, but he knew it was only a defense. She resented that he could read her every emotion, but he couldn't help it that she wore her heart on her sleeve for the world to see. That she did only further endeared her to him. Rough as she'd had it, she still felt, still needed, still wanted . . . yet she feared those very things. For some reason, she thought she didn't deserve them the way everyone else did.

And she was braced for some confrontation in a way that tore at his heart.

"Let's eat," he said with a little sigh, watching her visibly relax.

So he was forced to try to keep his eyes off her delectable body while they ate sandwiches, drank sodas, and laughed at the birds demanding crumbs. Nicole leaned forward to toss them chips, and his eyes feasted on her while he sipped his drink. Her no-nonsense swimsuit was cut neither high on the leg nor low in the front, but it fit her slim form sleekly enough to have him wanting to die of pleasure when a breeze made her obviously cold.

Two birds got especially brave, hopping close and screeching wildly for food. Nicole laughed as they raced each other on the sand, and Alex thought he couldn't think of a nicer sound than her sweet laughter.

"Candy told me you used to water-ski and that you were good enough to win a few championships," Nicole said suddenly. She tossed another chip to the birds, smiling when they came closer. "Do you still water-ski?"

She had to be told sooner or later, and he'd put it off too long. "My ex-fiancée's family owned the boat I used."

She dropped the chip she held. "Oh."

"It was years ago—"

"I didn't mean to pry."

He winced at the formal tone she used. "You didn't." He watched her carefully, trying to gauge her reaction. "Would you like to hear about it?"

"No," she said with a quick shake of her head, kneeling on her towel. "It's all right, Candy already told me."

He felt his eyebrows raise in surprise. She'd known all along and hadn't said a word about it. He thought of all the sleep he'd lost trying to figure out how to explain it to her. "It doesn't bother you?"

"Of course not," she said, still avoiding his gaze. "I'd be surprised if you hadn't had a serious relationship."

"Why?" he joked. "Because I'm so old?"

"You're hardly old," she said, giving him a look that had his blood racing. "It's just that you . . . you seem to . . . like women," she finished awkwardly.

He grinned and moved to her towel. "You noticed."

"This towel isn't big enough for both of us."

"Sure it is." He pulled her onto his lap and had to close his eyes as her warm skin came in contact with his. "How come *you* haven't married?"

She'd gone still as stone on him. "I'm still young."

He knew that defensive tone well, but ignored it as

he slid a finger over her cheek, amused at her discomfort. "Never found the right person," he asked, "or never looked?"

She batted his hand away and struggled to rise. "I'm ready to go back out in the water now."

He bet she was, but he stood too. "You know what I think? You've never given anyone the chance." He tipped her head up to look into her clear, amber eyes. "Give me that chance, Nicole."

"It's hot," she said on a choppy breath. "The water looks . . . really great."

"Nicole," he said, leaning closer, feeling intoxicated by the scent of her wet hair and sweet skin. "Tell me you're going to give this a chance, that you're going to see this crazy thing between us through."

"Crazy is the right word," she muttered, making him laugh.

But the laughter died in his throat when she lifted her lips to his softly. He made a low sound of surprise and reached for her, just as she reached for him. Their arms got tangled up in each other, and she backed away, clearly embarrassed. Laughing with delight, he pulled her back. "You kissed me," he said, surprised and happy. "You kissed *me*."

"So?" She scowled, crossing her arms. "I didn't realize you've never been kissed before."

"Not by you." God, her bare skin smelled good, and having it against his drove him crazy. He nudged her closer. "Do it again."

Hesitating, she lifted her lips chastely, her eyes flying open when he laughed. "*What?*" she demanded.

"Krista kisses me like that." He forced his hands to stay still on her waist, to be as passive as he could. "Come on, Nicole. *I dare you.*"

She gave him a wicked look and kissed him, and he went completely undone. Dizzy, hazy desire made his world spin. His heart followed. Pulling her closer, he reveled in the sensation, loving the feel of her arms wrapped tight around his neck, the silkiness of her hair brushing against his shoulders, the contrast of her cold, damp swimsuit and her sun-warmed skin.

The droning sound of an engine had them moving reluctantly apart. He touched the scrambling pulse at the base of her neck, aroused beyond belief. "We'd better go back out, before we—"

"Yes," Nicole agreed quickly, averting her eyes from him, and his swimming trunks that blatantly proved her kiss had been a rousing success. She ran like hell for the water.

Later Nicole could remember how peaceful the small cove seemed, how she loved driving the Waverunner with Alex holding her tight against him.

A small ski boat ripped across the water in front of them, its three male occupants laughing and singing at the top of their lungs. As the boat skimmed over the water like lightning, passing far too close to Alex and Nicole, the guys raised beer bottles in salute. Their wake nearly capsized the Waverunner.

Nicole held tight, fighting to stay on, and felt Alex do the same. "Did you see—"

"Idiots!" Alex said in disgust. "I hope the ranger catches them before they kill someone."

Idiots they be, Nicole thought grimly. But one of those idiots was her cousin Brad. She'd caught his surprised start of recognition as they'd passed, a brief instant before he'd urgently leaned to the driver of the boat and said something.

The boat, still gliding across the choppy water, turned in a wide arc before heading back toward them.

"Look out," Alex said angrily, tightening his hold on Nicole. "They're coming back for round two."

The boat passed them again, just as fast as before, but this time the triumphant howls were filled with derision. It took Alex less than a second to figure out why, and when he did, Nicole heard his long and colorful oath. She recognized Brad's two friends, Mark and Dan. They were his gambling buddies. Mark drove the boat, and Dan and Brad stood next to him. Dan and Mark obviously found the situation hilarious, but Brad now looked pale and sick. She watched as he again spoke urgently to the others, causing new peals of laughter.

Nicole had originally slowed and veered to the side, but Alex took the controls from her and did his best to get away from the boat. She must have made some sound of distress, because Alex took the time to rub his cheek against hers. "Lean with me in the turns, Nicole, that's it. Here they come again. Hold on."

She could feel the strain of his muscles as he leaned against her to manage the craft, could feel the tension coiled within him as he tried to get to the beach before the boat caught up with them. But they were no match for the speedboat. Mark came up on the side of the Waverunner, forcing them back toward the open water.

Nicole fought with all her strength to stay on. The wind had picked up, making the water naturally choppy, but with the maneuverings of the boat, the water churned like an ocean. Over and over again the boat circled them, and the water tossed and turned the Waverunner as if it were nothing more than a slight raft.

If Mark and Dan's expressions were any indicators, they were having the time of their lives. Nicole knew the most danger came from the fact that they were too drunk to gauge the distance between the boat and the Waverunner properly, and fear replaced her anger.

Brad gripped the dash of the boat, looking anxious, his eyes never leaving Nicole. The wind slid over Alex and Nicole's wet bodies. Her hands started to cramp from Alex's tight grip over hers and she shook with cold and fright.

The boat veered sharply and a swell washed over the Waverunner, leaving both Nicole and Alex gasping for air.

"Having fun?" Mark shouted over the roar of his boat.

Alex veered sharply to the left and gunned the gas while Nicole held her breath.

"Come on, Coleman," Mark called, teetering. "Show us what you're made of. Race us." He steered straight for the Waverunner. At the last minute he went to turn, smiling in anticipation, but either the craft didn't respond, or he was too drunk to manage the wheel.

With a sickening crunch, the two crafts collided.

The boat stayed upright and kept moving, but the Waverunner couldn't possibly withstand such a blow. It flipped twice, and Nicole watched in fascinated slow motion as she was ripped from Alex's arms by the impact. Clearing both crafts, she slammed into the water.

TWELVE

Nicole broke the surface, then stared in stunned disbelief at the boat racing away from them.

She heard her name called, as if from a great distance, and for a minute she stared blankly around her. What was she doing in the cold water alone? The million brilliant reflections of sun bounced off each whitecap, and she squinted painfully.

The unmanned Waverunner idled slowly past her, and she remembered. "Alex!" She whirled around, trying to see, then gasped at the sight of him ten feet from her, blood pouring down his face from a gash on his forehead. "Oh my God, your head!"

He paused and raised a hand to his head, staring dazedly as it came away red and sticky with his own blood. Nicole swam shakily toward him and straight into his arms, mindless of the blood that dripped all over her.

"You scared me to death," he said, hugging her to him fiercely. She clung to him, her heart skipping a beat when his hold on her loosened. His tan faded to a pasty gray as blood continued to flow from his head.

The Waverunner circled past them again, getting farther and farther away, and there wasn't another boat in sight. "Come on," she said, worried about how quiet he was. "Let's catch the Waverunner." Together they managed to swim to it, holding on to the side, gasping for breath.

But Alex hadn't spoken since his initial shout for her. Nicole suspected he was staying afloat mainly due to the life jacket he wore, and she tried not to panic, but it was hard. They were alone far from shore, and there was no help in sight.

"We have to get on," she said urgently to Alex. "Can you do it?"

His eyes remained glazed and dark. Nicole glanced frantically around them at the choppy water. A huge swell crashed over them, and she coughed and sputtered, then grabbed for Alex just as he lost his hold. "Alex!" She squeezed his arms. "Hold on." God, what was she going to do? "Get on, Alex. Please, get on."

He didn't respond at all this time, not even with a look, and her panic grew. "Alex, *please*." She tried to push him on, but his sheer size and deadweight were no match for her. Twice he tried to help her, but his hands slipped and he fell back into the water. She screamed his name as he slipped under before emerging to grasp weakly at the side of the Waverunner. The wound on his head gaped open and bled profusely, and Nicole knew he needed immediate medical attention. She shoved at him, crying earnestly now, and he tried to help. Somehow, between the two of them, he managed to get on. Scrambling up in front of him as quickly as she could, she panted big gulps of air and ignored the aches and pains beginning to make themselves known.

All she had to do now was drive for help. Simple enough.

But the engine wouldn't catch. Swiping tears and hair from her face, she tried again. No luck.

"Flooded," Alex mumbled against her shoulder.

Against her better judgment, Nicole tried again, filled with terror. This couldn't be happening. Alex couldn't possibly be bleeding as much as he was, her cousin couldn't possibly have left them to drown.

Then, a miracle. The Waverunner started. "Alex, can you hear me?" she demanded, her voice shaking. He didn't answer. He shouldn't be behind her, he wouldn't be able to hold on. But she knew she couldn't reach around him to control the Waverunner. "Alex. *Alex!*"

With eyes disturbingly vague and cloudy, he nodded. Or at least she thought he did. "I'm going to hit the gas," she said, with much more confidence than she felt. "You've got to hold on tight. Can you do that?" His hands tightened slightly around her waist.

The water rolled like an ocean, and the craft seemed to hit each crest harder than the last. Alex groaned softly against her shoulder, and her heart twisted in fear, fear motivated by the heavy flow of blood running down her shoulder and arm.

At this point Nicole wasn't sure which direction to head in, or where they had beached their things. Nothing looked familiar. All she knew was that they needed help—and quickly. So she headed toward the closest shore, which looked far, too far away.

They hit the next swell so bone-jarringly hard, it nearly dislodged them both. Alex's arms slackened. Whirling around, Nicole watched him slump back, and she screamed his name. When he didn't respond, she dropped the controls to grab at him, but a shout penetrated her concentration.

She looked up into the friendly eyes of a ranger, on a patrol boat idling alongside of her. It was small, but undoubtedly the most beautiful sight Nicole had ever seen. They lifted the unconscious Alex first, then Nicole. Within a few short minutes the two rangers had gotten Nicole's half-hysterical story, radioed for an ambulance to meet them at the launch, and ordered a backup to search for the boat that had hit them.

By now Nicole's limbs had turned to ice, and she couldn't stop shaking. The two rangers glanced at each other. "Shock," she heard one of them say as he wrapped blankets around her. She wanted to deny that, but she couldn't speak because suddenly her teeth were chattering. The drone of the engine bothered her, made her head hurt, and just for a second she closed her eyes.

The next thing she knew, she was being lifted into the ambulance next to Alex. He mumbled and turned his head toward her, his eyes flashing open. She sat straight up and groped for his hand, but his eyes closed again.

"Nicole," he whispered with faint accusation. "Don't leave."

The sight of him, usually so vital and active, now lying prone under a gray blanket splotched with his own blood, had her trembling all over again. "I'm not going anywhere," she told him, trying to keep her voice even. "We're just getting you to the doctor."

"No. Promise you won't leave me." He struggled to sit up, but a medic gently pushed him back. "Promise," he ground out. "Promise you won't leave."

He looked so huge on the narrow gurney. And helpless. "I promise, Alex." She'd stay by his side in the hospital.

But even that small promise, made in good faith, was meant to be broken. At the hospital they were separated. Nicole got checked out in the emergency room for shock, a sprained ankle, and a bloody lip. She tried to see Alex, but was told she couldn't until after the doctor had finished with him. When they wouldn't tell her his condition, she huddled on her bed, trying not to panic.

He hadn't lost as much blood as it seemed, she tried to convince herself. Besides, head wounds always bled like a stuck pig. Everyone knew that.

Though she hadn't wanted to worry anyone, she called the inn and left a message for Susan, hoping someone would come and bring her clothes, since all she had was a blanket and a bathing suit.

It was quite possible she was going to kill Brad.

But some of her anger drained when she thought of her cousin's horrified face the split second before impact. Then the curtain to her cubicle flew open and Candy rushed in, her eyes filled with worry. "Nicole," she cried, running forward and grabbing her in a hug. "What happened?"

Nicole's face was pressed against her aunt, her body squeezed tight. She couldn't speak if she'd wanted to, but for a second the offered comfort was too much to resist and she didn't try. It didn't matter that the woman had held back with her, it didn't matter that Nicole couldn't trust her. All that mattered in that instant was that Nicole needed and Candy gave, no questions asked. Was that what being family meant, then?

Without a bit of warning, Nicole was sobbing in Candy's arms, uncertain if she was crying for Alex or herself.

"Oh honey," Candy said, holding her close. "I'm so

sorry, so sorry. Susan called me, frantic, because she couldn't get away. I came as fast as I could."

Nicole could only cry harder.

"Nicole, it's going to be all right now." She gestured helplessly at the bag of clothes she'd brought. "Let me help you dress, maybe you can tell me what happened."

She didn't dress because it felt so good to have Candy holding her, but she did tell the story. When she got to the part about Brad's involvement, she faltered. "I'm sorry," she whispered, seeing both the collision and Brad's terrified expression all over again.

"At least he wasn't driving the boat," Candy said, shaking her head. "It certainly doesn't excuse him, but I don't think he can be arrested."

"There's more," Nicole told her. "He's been stealing money from the inn, and I think he's gambling. Heavily." Candy stared at her, and Nicole was disgusted enough by the family's lack of communication and unity to spill the rest. "Susan knows. She's been putting the money back into the inn from her own pocket to cover it, but she's broke."

"What did Alex do about the money missing from the inn?" Candy gasped when Nicole grimaced guiltily. "Oh, Nicole. I can see why Susan didn't dare tell him. But why couldn't you?"

"I should have. I wanted to," Nicole said earnestly. "I was going to tell him today, as soon as we got back from the lake. I held off because I thought Brad would stop, I thought Susan would be more careful." She let her shoulders slump in defeat. She'd been wrong, terribly wrong. "I worried about what it would do to Brad."

"I had no idea," Candy said quietly. "I'm sure Ted has no idea, though he should."

"Brad needs help. Now more than ever. He's got to turn himself in. That would be a start."

They sat together and worried, and when Nicole was cleared by the doctor to go, she refused.

"I can't go until they tell me about Alex," she said firmly to Candy. She glanced through the closed doors to the operating center and wrapped the blanket tighter around her shoulders. Please, she prayed, please let him be all right.

Unfortunately for Alex, he came to just as they started stitching him up. The needle that stuck into his open wound had him gritting his teeth against a powerful wave of nausea that wouldn't quit. Sweat dripped off him. The doctor pulled back, barking out orders to his nurse. Alex relaxed slightly—until the doctor turned back to him, another needle in hand.

"Okay," the doctor announced cheerfully, "you'll be numb in a minute. Clean wound. It shouldn't scar too badly."

This time when he waved the needle, Alex's vision faded mercifully to black.

When he came to, he lay still, taking inventory of his pains. There were many. Gingerly, he flexed his arms and legs, then brought a hand up to his throbbing head. And remembered.

"Nicole." He sat straight up, then nearly passed out again from the sharp pain the sudden movement caused.

"Well, well." A nurse appeared in his vision. "You're back with us. How do you feel?"

As if he was about to throw up everywhere. "Nicole," he said again, licking his chapped lips. He'd never felt more thirsty or more frightened in his entire life. "Where is she?"

"I'm here."

He turned, the relief he'd felt draining at the sight of her curled in the chair next to his bed.

"I'll be back with the doctor," the nurse said, leaving them alone.

Alex's eyes didn't leave Nicole, but his stomach tightened painfully. Her hair stuck to one side of her head with what looked suspiciously like blood—his, he fervently hoped. Wrapped in a blanket, her feet tucked beneath her, her arms pulled tight in front of her, she looked small, vulnerable, and very frightened. Too pale, he thought, and those lips he loved to kiss were positively blue. What the hell's wrong with these people? he wondered angrily. Anyone could see how cold she was. And those wide, gold eyes held worry, sorrow, and . . . pain.

He wanted to rise and hold her, but he'd throw up if he moved a muscle. "Are you hurt?"

To his surprise, her eyes filled with tears. "Oh, Alex, you scared me," she whispered, rising. She struggled with the blanket, then leaned over him.

He grabbed her hand, reassured when she squeezed it tight. He had to stay calm, but it was damned difficult when she looked so awful. "Where are you hurt, Nicole?"

She shook her head. "I'm not. Not as badly as you."

He tugged until she sat next to him. "Where?" he demanded.

"Just a sprained ankle. That's all."

He brought a finger to her swollen lip, wincing when she did. He wished he could banish the haunted, tense look from her eyes. "Those bastards are going to pay for this, I promise you."

But when Nicole blanched, he immediately regretted the outburst. Clenching his jaw against the pain, Alex wove his fingers through her tangled hair, tilting her head down so he could see into her eyes. "You saw, too, didn't you. You know it was Brad."

"Yes." Startling him, she grasped his shoulders and leaned close. "Alex, I need to tell you something very important. I—"

"Alex," Susan said sharply from the door, her eyebrows shooting up in surprise at the sight of Nicole leaning over him. Nicole straightened, then got herself tangled in the blanket she still wore as she eased back to the chair, looking defeated.

Alex could have cheerfully strangled Susan for the interruption. But he felt too weak, and the pounding in his head wouldn't ease. Leaning back, he had to close his eyes. "What is it, Susan?"

"I'm sorry, Nicole," Susan said carefully, eyeing her cousin. "I thought you were changing. Candy told me what happened." She turned to Alex. "I see you're fine."

"Sorry to disappoint you," he said dryly.

"I was asking sincerely."

It hurt to talk. "Don't bother with the false sympathy, it doesn't become you."

"Look, Alex," Susan said, her tone tightening a little. "No matter what's happened in the past, I don't want to see you hurt. Or anyone else for that matter."

"Ah," he said, opening his eyes and narrowing them on her. "I see what this is about. You're worried about Brad."

"Alex—" Nicole started, struggling to rise.

"Nicole, wait." Susan came farther into the room. "I

know I interrupted you, and I'm sorry, but this is very important. It'll only take a minute. Krista's watching the inn for me, and I have to get back."

Alex watched warily as Susan stepped up to his bed. He'd swear she was up to something big, but what, he couldn't imagine.

Nicole stood, looking wobbly. "I'll just change, then, give you two a minute."

"No, Nicole, don't leave. You already know about this and you can help me explain."

Alex glanced curiously at Nicole, shocked to see her go at least three shades whiter, if that were possible. Dread filled him.

"Alex," Susan said quietly and quickly. "Brad has been taking money from the Wilson House. I put most of it back, but when Nicole discovered it while doing the books, I panicked and tried to cover for him. I thought it was the right thing to do, and now today, I see I was wrong. He needs help." She paused, her eyes lit with honesty when she added, "I'm sorry, Alex."

Alex's stunned eyes settled on Nicole, who was busy studying the ceiling tiles. His head felt as if it had a train running through it as he turned back to Susan. "Why didn't you tell me?"

She shrugged. "I thought I could handle it. I thought I was helping him."

A part of him felt only relief. For some time he'd known something was wrong with the books, and he and his accountant had been on the verge of discovering what. But the other part of him knew only pain, pain that had nothing to do with the accident. He looked at Nicole, not realizing how he felt until she flinched at his expression.

His stomach roiled as though he'd been punched.

Brad and Susan had been messing with the books of his business, and Nicole had known. *She hadn't told him.* It was a bitter pill to swallow.

"You knew," he stated carefully, keeping his tone even. She nodded, and the fear in her eyes made him want to smash something. It put him over the edge, knowing she expected him to retaliate. Hadn't he proven himself to her yet? "Susan," he said, feeling mean and nasty, and sick with pain, "how much do you and your sorry brother still owe me?"

"Five hundred dollars."

It was an effort to speak. "I'll expect it back by tomorrow. If not, I'm filing charges. Krista will take all the financial information with her. It will no longer be in your control. Got it?"

"Got it," she said softly, bitterly, then turned on her heel and walked to the door. "Nicole?" Her eyes warmed and she held out a hand. "Coming?"

"Nicole and I aren't finished talking yet," Alex said, grinding his teeth so hard he was surprised he had any left.

Susan looked at Nicole, but Nicole only shook her head. Susan shrugged and left.

"I thought we were friends," he managed to say past the roaring in his head, past the pain and betrayal.

"We are," she said, leaning forward on the chair. "I—"

"No," he said harshly, closing his eyes again. Damn, he hurt. "You'll *never* convince me you believed that. It just isn't the truth. You've resisted it the entire time you've been here. I really should be tired of trying by now." He sighed, his heart aching. "Nicole, if nothing else, I'm your boss. You had no right to keep the fact that an employee was stealing from me."

She said nothing, but pulled the pathetic blanket closer around her, unable to hide a shiver. A bruise on her cheek was darkening. Looking at her should have defused his anger, but instead, irrationally, it fueled it. She didn't believe in him, and never had. "Get dressed," he snapped, overcome by unaccustomed bitterness and loss. Why hadn't they made sure she got dressed? "Go home."

Nicole didn't know if Alex meant for her to actually leave town or to go back to the inn, but she did neither. Emotions raw, she sat waiting outside his cubicle in the emergency room. He emerged over an hour later, wearing scrubs, and stared at her.

She'd never been more aware of her appearance. She'd long since changed into the jeans Candy had brought, but without a shower there wasn't much she could do about the blood still stuck in her hair.

"Why are you still here?" he asked gruffly, walking past her with a carefully navigated gait that spoke of his pain.

"I'm taking you home." She hoped she sounded firmer than she felt. Her knees wobbled as he cocked an eyebrow at her.

"You're not taking me anywhere."

Okay, so he was still furious, he had a right to be. But she'd make it up to him, she had to. She was going to take him home. Thanks to a friend of Candy's, Alex's Blazer was at the hospital.

Alex walked away, slowly, as if each footstep was agony. It probably was—he had a multitude of stitches, a slight concussion, and a bottle of pain pills in his hand that he hadn't yet opened. Nothing worse than a man mad *and* in pain, she acknowledged, knowing from personal experience. And she'd caused both.

Still, he walked away from her. Holding up her hand, she jingled his car keys. That got his attention. Stopping, he turned back to her, eyeing the keys with narrowed eyes. She recognized the stubborn look and resigned herself to a fight.

"I'm driving you home," she said again, firmly.

"Fine," he said, surprising her. Looking too weary to argue, he made his way toward the door without a backward glance.

She tried to be grateful he'd given in so quickly, tried not to be alarmed at how he'd looked at her. It would get better.

It didn't.

Outside the Blazer, Alex turned a glacial look on her, and she thought he wanted the keys. "I'm driving," she said defensively. "You couldn't possibly—"

"Just unlock the damn door, Nicole," he said tiredly, leaning against the Blazer as if his own weight were too much for him.

She did, feeling like an idiot. Alex sank into the passenger seat with a groan, hooked his seat belt, reclined the seat, and closed his eyes.

He didn't say another word, didn't even move, and by the time she pulled up his driveway, Nicole assumed he'd fallen asleep. She leaned over him, her hand outstretched to wake him, when he spoke, making her jump.

"Take the Blazer back to the inn. Don't walk on your ankle."

That he cared had her heart pumping ridiculously fast. That he still didn't open his eyes or move a muscle had her anxious. "No."

He slitted an eye open. "No?" he asked in the tone

of someone who wasn't used to having an order disobeyed.

"I'm helping you inside."

"No, you're not." But he didn't budge. "Just give me a minute."

She got out of the Blazer, her ankle only giving her a twinge of pain. She opened his door, but he still didn't move. In fact, he sat so still, his breathing so even, she thought this time he *had* to be asleep. Slipping her arm around his shoulders, she gently pulled. "Come on, Alex," she said softly. "Let's go."

"I'm not asleep," he mumbled, sounding irritated. "And I'll get in by myself." But he came docilely enough and let her lead him up the stairs. Halfway up, she tripped, and Alex's arm tightened around her. And she realized with a heaviness in her chest caused by emotion, he hadn't once let her take on his full weight.

At his door, he took his keys, opened the lock, then handed the keys back to her. Obviously, she was dismissed.

THIRTEEN

Nicole watched Alex take his stairs with slow, deliberate steps. Ignoring his dismissal, she quietly followed him in.

When the shower started she cringed, thinking that he shouldn't be getting his head wet so soon. She also imagined that the anesthesia must be wearing off and the pain would soon be unbearable for him. But the pain pills lay in the sink where he'd tossed them as he entered.

Driven by a need she didn't understand, she moved around in the kitchen, fixing a tray with tea, crackers, and the pills, hoping he'd take a dose. Then she stood there, holding the tray, indecisive.

She should leave, just as he wanted. It'd certainly be easy, he'd seen to that.

But she wanted his trust back, and suddenly she'd do anything to get it. No one had ever trusted her the way he had, and she felt the loss more than she thought possible. So she trudged up the stairs, heart in her throat at the idea of him dismissing her again.

In his bedroom, she drank in her fill, her eyes settling

on the huge, rumpled bed. She wanted to be in there, with him, and the longing was so deep and so real, she staggered to a chair, put the tray down on the floor, and sat. It took her a second to realize the bathroom was ominously silent.

"Alex?"

He didn't answer, and she leaped to her feet, envisioning him passed out on the cold floor, bleeding to death. "Alex!" She knocked frantically. "Alex! Answer me!" She pounded on the door, about to rip it off its hinges when the handle moved. It slowly opened to reveal Alex leaning against the jamb, a towel wrapped low on his hips, his face ashen, his eyes glazed.

"Don't," he said hoarsely, squeezing his eyes shut. He braced his forehead and arm on the wall. "Please . . . don't."

"Don't what?"

"Make noise."

"I'm taking you to bed," she announced in her firmest voice.

But she still blushed a deep red when he lifted his head and sent her a dry look. "You might be disappointed."

She doubted that. Standing there with his dark, wet hair hanging over his forehead, his bruised and rangy body nearly nude, he looked like a Greek god. She wanted him, she realized with some surprise. She wanted him as she'd never wanted anyone before. Too bad he could hardly stand the sight of her. "Where are your clothes?"

He hitched his shoulder toward a pair of jogging shorts lying on the sink in the bathroom. Nicole grabbed them and, with a deep breath, bent down so he could step into them. His stormy eyes met hers. "I can dress myself, dammit." But he gripped the doorway as if he could hardly stand, and she could see the sweat beaded on his forehead from the effort.

"Humor me," she suggested lightly, holding the shorts open as he stepped into them. The towel slipped off, and she had to swallow hard, but even so, she couldn't force her gaze away. He was still angry at her, but from her angle, he definitely wasn't immune to her. He pulled up his shorts by himself, which was a good thing since she couldn't move. Both of them were riveted to the spot by a mutual magnetic attraction they couldn't shake.

Finally, Alex pushed past her and staggered to the bed, gingerly setting himself down on top of the tousled bedcoverings. Nicole stood over him, her fingers itching to help him straighten them out. He stretched out on his back, one arm thrown over his eyes.

Nicole stood there for long minutes, staring at the soft rise and fall of his still-damp chest. When he spoke, she nearly leaped out of her skin.

"Are you going to watch me sleep?"

"You're still mad."

"Hell, yes." He raised his arm off his eyes. "Did you think I wouldn't be?"

"I—"

"I *trusted* you." He let his arm fall back over his eyes. "I thought you trusted me."

The hurt in his voice gave her hope. She couldn't hurt someone who didn't care. "I was going to tell you."

"Not that I believe you, but when?"

"Today. At the lake." A facetious sound escaped him, and she hurried on. "I knew I couldn't keep it from you, I knew it was wrong. But we were having so much fun there, I didn't want to ruin it. I didn't want you to think

I'd done it to hurt you or misguide you. Then, in the hospital, I started to tell you, but Susan beat me to it."

"I see," he said quietly.

"Do you really?"

"Yes."

She wished he'd open his eyes and look at her, wished he'd sit up and offer to hold her. "I made tea."

"No thanks."

She moved to the bed, wanting to brush his hair from his face, wanting to lie against his side. She knew without a doubt, she could love this man, if she let herself. "Will you take a painkiller?"

"Later." He opened an eye. "Go back to the inn, Nicole. You need rest too." His tone softened. "You must be exhausted."

Her heart warmed at the way his voice gentled. "I'm not leaving you. I don't think you should be alone."

"I'll be fine. Go rest. Please."

"Later." He didn't respond, and she sat quietly on the bed, waiting for him to object. He didn't and she reached out to touch his cheek. "I'm so sorry, Alex. I never meant for this to happen, never meant to hurt you. I should have told you, wanted to tell you, but I'd promised. Then I was going to tell you anyway, I just didn't know how. Please, don't be mad anymore. . . . I want you to trust me again."

He said nothing and her heart sank a little. "Alex?" He'd fallen asleep.

Alex awoke with a start. The oak ceiling fan whirling gently above him told him he was in his own bed. The throbbing ache in his head reminded him of what had happened.

His eyes searched the room, then settled on Nicole, fast asleep in his large chair. Sitting there with her bare feet curled beneath her, wearing jeans and a T-shirt, sans makeup, she looked young, small, and incredibly desirable. Her hair was damp and minus the blood.

Picturing her in his shower did strange things to him. He recognized the lust for what it was, but had to admit, he'd never felt it give quite such a punch before.

Even as his body tightened in response to her, his heart clenched at her betrayal. She'd purposely deceived him. Knowing that, he still wished for the strength to go get her and bring her back to his bed.

Her eyes flew open and she stared at him, looking disoriented. "What time is it?" she whispered.

"I don't know," he whispered back.

She glanced at his clock. "It's five. You only slept half an hour."

"How would you know? You were asleep."

She straightened. "I was not."

"You were."

She narrowed her eyes, obviously trying to figure out why he was using that teasing tone when he was supposed to be so angry at her. Her confusion sobered him quickly enough. She'd had a lifetime of people walking away from her. She fully expected him to do the same.

When she stretched, then winced, he rose cautiously to his elbows. "You okay?"

"Fine," she said, too quickly.

Alex pushed himself upright, grimacing against the wave of pain. "Tell me the truth," he berated her. "You ache from head to toe, just as I do."

"Wait—what are you doing?" she demanded as he rose from the bed. "Don't get up, you'll get dizzy."

She was right, he thought as the room swayed and he tilted crazily. He felt her arms slide around his waist.

"What do you think you're doing?" she cried, and he could hear annoyance and panic in her voice.

He rested his chin on top of her head, adjusting her in his arms so that she didn't bear his weight, and he tried not to notice how right it felt to hold her in his arms again. "I wanted to get you up from that chair and take you back to the inn so you could rest."

"Oh."

Even with her face pressed against his chest, he could hear her disappointment. But he couldn't give in, and let her rest here. If he did, he'd probably do something humiliating—like beg her to give him what he wanted. Trying to disentangle himself, he found her holding him with the tenacity of a bulldog.

"I've got to sit, Nicole," he said gently. Lord, even his legs shook.

He managed to back them to the bed before they both fell across it, Nicole splayed across his chest, her hands clinging to his shoulders.

And he remembered.

He suddenly remembered in vivid detail how she'd threatened, cajoled, and finally, had frantically begged him to get on the Waverunner so she could get him help. He tightened his hands on her waist. "I never thanked you for what you did today," he said huskily. "I—"

"You are *not* going to thank me." She pushed off him, tried to lever away, but he caught her.

But for a minute he could only stare, struggling with the picture of the shy, petite woman in his arms being the same one who had demanded and bullied him to safety. She'd also lied to him and sided against him. And yet, strangely enough, he felt he could understand. Without a birth certificate, she felt confused and alone. She had no idea who she was, had no sense of identity. She wanted family, and she wanted the loyalty and unconditional love that went with it. If only he could make her see she could get that from someone *besides* family. From someone like him.

He was losing it. He needed to think—and he couldn't do that with those large, beautiful whiskey eyes of hers on him. He gently forced her over and sat up, wincing. "Let's call Candy to come get you."

"Now?"

Was that a panicky edge to her voice? Her eyes were wide and stunned, her hair tousled. Her breath came fast. "Yes," he said in a voice rougher than he meant. "If I keep you here, I'll break my promise to you." And he reached for the telephone next to the bed, not taking his eyes off her.

Almost desperate, she yanked him back. Unable to help himself, he closed his arms tight around her and buried his face in her hair. "Nicole, don't," he said softly, desperately. "I can't keep watching you walk away, it's killing me."

Her eyes squeezed shut as she pulled back. "I'm sorry."

Quietly, he got Candy on the phone, pausing while he listened to her worried ramblings.

And Nicole, upset as she was, saw him freeze, felt his horror.

When he hung up, he reached for her hand, eyes unusually solemn. "Brad's missing."

"Nicole, honey, wake up."

Nicole blinked, groaned at the aches in her body, and turned away from the light. "Go away, Susan."

"I know it's early. But I have to talk to you. Please?"

From where she lay, her face buried in her pillow, Nicole sighed. "Did Brad turn up yet?"

"No. It's not that. Please, Nicole? Can we talk?"

With another groan, Nicole flipped over and squinted at the clock by her bed. After everything that had happened the day before, she hadn't expected to sleep well, but she had. "I don't really want to talk to you right now."

"You're mad at me for telling Alex about the missing money."

Every muscle screamed in resistance to the thought of rising. "I don't understand why you told him that way, after you'd sworn me to secrecy." She looked at her cousin, but Susan's face was carefully blank.

"He was bound to be furious, no matter who told him. Besides, it was my duty, no one else's."

Nicole had wondered at the seemingly selfish and premeditated gesture before she'd fallen asleep. "Why was it *your* duty?"

Susan fidgeted, an unusual movement that had Nicole on alert. "Let's just say," Susan murmured, "we have a history. And I owed him."

"History?"

"I didn't want to tell you, Nicole. It's embarrassing, really."

"Spill it, Susan."

She sighed heavily before admitting, "I was engaged to Alex once."

Susan's next words were lost as Nicole remembered so many little things that suddenly made sense. Alex and

Susan's strange animosity. Candy alluding to the engagement. Alex had tried to tell her, but she'd brushed it off. "Engaged," she repeated stupidly.

"A long time ago. This is really tough to admit, but I was young and *very* stupid." Her eyes were shadowed by humiliation. "I'd had a crush on him forever. He was the most gorgeous guy in town. Definitely the most sophisticated."

Nicole closed her eyes. Alex and Susan. "Why didn't you marry him, Susan?"

"Oh, I wanted to," she said, her voice faint with remembered bitterness. "But he wouldn't have me. He caught me with his best friend."

Nicole's eyes flew open. "You cheated on him?"

Susan nodded miserably. "Pretty dumb. Anyway, he couldn't forgive me and it's just as well."

"Why's that?" Nicole asked warily. "And why are you telling me this now?"

Susan reached for Nicole's hand. "He never loved me, Nicole. Not the adult kind of love. And to be completely honest with you, I've been trying to torture him all these years for that. That's why I told him yesterday. Just to be mean."

Nicole looked at her, disappointed and disillusioned.

"It was sick and pathetic," Susan said, reading her mind. "But until I saw the way you two looked at each other yesterday, I didn't realize it. By hurting him, I hurt you. Nicole, I've come to love you—no, I mean it. I never meant to hurt you. I just didn't know."

"You used me to hurt Alex."

"Yes, I did. I'm so sorry, Nicole, but while I'm being honest I have to tell you the rest. I invited you here in the beginning because I thought Maddie had left you a rich woman. I had high hopes of forcing Alex out of the inn. With your money."

"I see." Nicole pulled her hand free. "That's why you let me help you with the lease."

"Yes, only I didn't realize until recently that you have no more money than I do."

She felt sick. "And you're telling me this now because . . . ?"

"I don't want any more secrets between us. Alex doesn't want me and he never will, and Nicole, please believe me, I want you in my life. Without your money."

Nicole forced herself to sit up. Anger, betrayal, confusion, and sorrow hit her at once, leaving her restless. "I don't know what to say to you."

Susan's eyes glowed with regret. "Say you'll forgive me for the deceit. Believe that I want you here because I want you, not your inheritance. And believe that I really had no idea until yesterday that you and Alex had feelings for each other."

Nicole thought about how she'd betrayed Alex the same way Susan had betrayed her. And how he'd made Candy come get her rather than keep her with him. For the first time in maybe forever she panicked over the loss of someone close. "He's not exactly thrilled with me—"

"Oh, yes, he is." Susan held up her hand. "I know what I saw. I might still feel a twinge of jealousy now and again, it's in my blood. But I want you to be happy, Nicole. I mean it."

"I'm supposed to believe this?"

"Yes," her cousin said quietly. "You are. Because it's the truth. Are you going to stay and be my friend, my cousin, my family? I want that so badly. We have a lot left to do, you and I. We still have to find Brad and straighten him out. I'm ready to face that now, but I need your help, your strength."

Her strength? This strong woman needed *her?* Okay, maybe she was a fool, but she wanted to believe it. Desperately. And since she so fully understood what was behind the deceit—pure desperation—it was easy to forgive. "I'll stay, Susan. For the rest of the summer, just like I said I would."

"What about after—"

"*No after,*" Nicole said firmly, unable and unwilling to see that far into the future. "First, we'll find Brad."

Susan hugged her close. "I'm so sorry. I do love you, Nicole."

Nicole went still for a minute before hugging Susan back. "I know."

And the funny thing was, she did.

Nicole sat in front of the roaring fire in the Wilson House, studying the pictures of her family. Her *adoptive* family, she reminded herself.

They looked alike—Candy, Ella, and Ted. In fact, Candy and Ella could have been twins— She jumped to her feet, rooted to the spot by the answer that had been there all along.

Candy had said she was ten years Ella's junior, yet in this picture Ella couldn't have been more than twelve. That would mean Candy should be two, not the preteen she looked. *Candy was her mother.* The answer had been right there all along. Legs weak, she sank to her knees on the floor. The fire crackled enticingly, letting off a warm heat Nicole couldn't feel. Chilled, numb, and close to tears, she tossed the picture to the fire, flinching as it popped loudly.

Knowing that her own mother was too ashamed to claim her caused a pain so great, she thought she'd die right there. Nobody wanted her. Brad had left her for dead, Susan had her own motivation for everything. Ted couldn't care less, and Alex . . . well, she'd blown that, hadn't she? Three days had passed. He obviously had no intention of forgiving and forgetting anytime soon.

Suddenly her skin burned from being too close to the fire. Yet she felt like ice from the inside out. She shivered with it, even as her vision wavered and grayed.

FOURTEEN

Alex walked into the inn, tensed and coiled. He hadn't slept well, hadn't worked well, hadn't done anything well since he'd watched Candy take Nicole from his house. He didn't know what the hell to do, but knew he had to do something—or go crazy.

Then his heart stopped at the sight of Nicole slumped on the floor, too close to the fireplace. Running to her, he scooped her into his lap, cradling her against him. "Nicole. Baby, come on, wake up." He shook her gently, then squeezed her in relief when her eyes fluttered open.

"Alex?"

"It's me." He held her tight against him when she would have gotten up, his heart racing against hers. "Wait a minute, just hold still. What happened? Are you hurt?"

She shook her head slowly. "I don't think so. I must have passed out for a second."

She felt clammy and so fragile in his arms. How

could he have forgotten that? She trembled, and he hugged her close. "What is it?"

But she shook her head. "I'm fine," she whispered, dropping her gaze. Then she pushed from his lap and stood shakily. "I'm sorry."

"*Sorry?*" She'd shut him out—again. His anger rose as he did. "You fainted and you're sorry?" How easy it was for rage to smooth over the heart-stopping panic he'd felt at the sight of her lying too still on the floor. "What the hell's going on?"

"You don't need this, Alex. Really you don't."

"Don't tell me what I need. Sit down before you fall again. Now, dammit," he said unkindly as she wavered. He pushed her on the couch and knelt before her, holding her arms. "Look at me. *At me.*" When she did, he saw her eyes, nearly all black, with just a hint of an amber circle. Shock, he thought, and his anger drained to be replaced by fear. "Nicole, please, talk to me."

"You're . . . not still mad?"

The catch in her voice did something to him. Cursing himself for making her wait, for letting her think he'd walked away from her, he sighed deeply. "You hurt me, Nicole. And I got mad. You apologized and I got over it. That's how this thing works between us. I stayed away because that's what you wanted."

"You still like me."

He hated that unsure hesitation, and wanted to go back in time to take care of each and every person who had ever hurt her as a child. He couldn't, but he *could* help the woman. "I love you, Nicole."

Her eyes went so wide, he could see white all around the amber circles. "You—I've got to sit down, Alex."

"You are sitting down," he pointed out. She looked

even sicker now and he found he could laugh. "This isn't quite the reaction I pictured, Nicole."

"I can't breathe," she muttered, breathing just fine.

"Do you always get sick when someone says I love you?"

Head dropped in her hands, her voice came muffled. "No one's ever said it before."

Which explained a lot and had his heart aching all the more. "Well, I just did. I'll say it again if you want. I—"

"No!" Panicky, she lifted her head and put her fingers over his lips. "Once was enough, really. Thank you."

He tried not to be disappointed, but it was difficult. "The point is, you're stuck with me." He waited until her breathing evened out and her color returned. "Tell me what upset you."

"I can't think now."

"Try."

"Candy's my mother. And she's too ashamed of me to admit it."

He stared at her. "That's not true."

"Then why can't they tell me?"

He watched those beautiful eyes fill and felt her pain as his own. "I don't know, but it has nothing to do with you, you've got to believe that."

Taking her icy hands in his, he brought them up to his mouth to warm them.

Finally he understood why she believed herself so unworthy of love. *She believed no one wanted her, that no one could.* After all, her own mother had been within reach this entire time.

How could he show this beautiful, hurting woman she deserved love like everyone else?

By showing her how very much she was wanted, desired, loved. Cupping her face, he drew her near and kissed her. He kissed her until he felt her relax and lean into him, until he heard the little murmur of helpless desire in her throat. It was all the invitation he needed to lift her in his arms and head for the stairs, where he intended not to stop until he was in her room making love to her. Showing her how much he wanted her, needed her, loved her.

"Nicole."

With Nicole still in his arms, Alex turned to see Susan. "She's busy," he said, starting up the stairs.

"It's Brad," Susan said in a funny voice that had him stopping again. "He's . . . well, the police found him in Reno, as we suspected. Brad panicked and ran. There was a chase."

Nicole made a sound of dismay, and Alex let go of her knees so she could slide down to stand. "Get to the point, Susan," he said, frustrated.

"He wrapped his car around a tree, Alex," Susan snapped, in a rare show of emotion. "Is that close enough to the point?"

Nicole brought her hands to her mouth. "Oh, God. No."

Susan's face twisted. "And he's in the hospital, unconscious. That's all they'd tell me. I'm going to him now."

"I'm coming with you," Nicole said tersely, giving Alex a look he understood all too well.

Clearly, she blamed herself and Alex for all of it.

Alex waited, tight-lipped and tense, as John Mitchell walked through the finished day-care center with his clipboard in hand. John's eyes darted left and right, and his pencil flew across the paper.

Useless as it was, Alex stood watching, seeped in anger.

Krista, from her perch on the windowsill, sent Alex a glance of sympathy.

"Passed," John said.

"What?" Alex glanced in surprise at his sister.

She jumped down to move to Alex's side, then took his hand and squeezed it. "Just like that?"

"Just like that." John handed him his slip and left.

Krista hugged Alex. He forced himself to relax and hugged his sister back.

"You did good," she whispered.

"I can't believe it. After all the trouble I've had with him, I thought for sure he'd fail us."

"I know, honey, I know. He's just a bully. Pay no attention."

Alex smiled, just as she'd meant him to. She'd been protecting him—or trying to—since he'd been born.

It was ironic that the thing that had meant the most to him for so long—his expansion—meant nothing without Nicole.

"Alex," Krista said, watching him worriedly. "Tell me about her. Maybe I can help."

It was useless to be surprised by her insight. "Not this time you can't." He closed his eyes against the raw pain of it. Forget his expansion, forget the damn daycare. All he wanted was Nicole.

"You love her."

His heart clenched. He wanted her, desperately. The rest of this would be a snap if she were here, by his side. "Yeah, I love her. We belong together, though she doesn't believe it. There's nothing more I can do."

She smiled wistfully. "You work hard, Alex, and you're a good man. The best. But there's one way you're terribly spoiled." His head snapped up, but she only shook hers. "Things come easy to you," she told him gently. "They always have."

"But nothing's meant as much as this. As much as her."

She smiled. "Then it's worth the work."

"There's nothing more I can do," he repeated helplessly.

She looked at him. "There's always more we can do."

She was right, of course. Feeling his frustration mount into anger, he whipped out of the parking lot and onto the main highway. He didn't stop until he sat out front of the one person's house who could turn this around for him.

Candy opened her door, looking surprised. "Alex. I just got back from the hospital. Brad's still in a coma. Come in?"

He shook his head. "Nicole's in bad shape, Candy."

That shocked her into momentary silence. "I just saw her. She looked fine."

"Fine isn't good, dammit." He struggled with his temper and reminded himself that he genuinely liked this woman in front of him. "She won't let me near her, and she's confused, hurt, and feeling completely alone."

Candy's eyes turned wary. She pulled back a step. "Why are you telling me this?"

"I think you know why." Candy bit her lip in a gesture so reminiscent of Nicole, he sighed. Softening his voice, he said, "Please, Candy, tell her. It isn't right to keep it, not when it's gone this far."

"You're hurting her," he added when she remained silent, her eyes glistening.

"You haven't . . . said anything?"

"Not yet. Tell her, Candy. Tell her," he said quietly. "Or you'll lose her forever. We all will."

Nicole needed closure. Without it, her life was on hold. She was risking everything; her happiness, her sanity . . . Alex.

Before she knew what she was doing, she'd driven to Ted's office and asked to be seen.

Ted smiled when he entered, though the smile didn't quite reach his eyes. He looked gaunt and pale, in complete contrast to his considerable girth, and the nervous strain about him transferred itself immediately to her. "I've been waiting for you."

"Oh, no." She lurched out of her chair. "Brad? Is he—"

"No," he said quickly. "It's not Brad. There's been no change." He hesitated. "I'm worried about you, Nicole. So's Candy."

"Then she should come tell me herself." When Ted took a deep breath, she felt her temper explode. "For God's sake, I know I'm adopted. What I want to know is, are you prepared to give me the answers I want?"

To his credit, he didn't hedge or hesitate. "I'm not the one they should come from."

Candy.

"You still have the file."

Startled by his uncharacteristic bluntness, and angry at herself for forgetting that she still had the file hidden under her mattress, she was at a complete loss for words.

"Nicole," he suggested gently. "Let's be honest."

"That, at least, would be a welcome change," she whispered.

He smiled, his first one. "I never leave my keys out. It's a cardinal rule with me."

She took in the special light in his eyes. "You left them out on purpose. *You've been sending me the letters.* Why?"

"You deserved to know, but it wasn't my decision to make. It wasn't my right to tell you."

"At first I thought you might have been my father."

"I would have been proud," he said simply, bringing tears to her eyes. "Just give her a chance, give her some more time. Everything will make better sense after you speak with her, I promise."

She had to take his word on that, but not for long since she drove straight to Candy's house and rang the bell. There was no answer.

Not about to turn around when she was all revved up for the confrontation of her life, she called out and entered. Storm clouds had rolled in, darkening the late afternoon. She found Candy in a back bedroom, surrounded by boxes, so intent on her work, she hadn't heard Nicole.

"Candy? Are you all right?"

Candy jumped nervously and quickly stuffed something back into the box in front of her. "Oh, Nicole," she forced a small smile as she turned, shielding that particular box. "You startled me. I got caught up in this stuff and lost track of time."

"What are you doing?"

"Ted and I decided to have an estate sale with our mother's things. Should have done it a long time ago . . ." Her laugh seemed forced, nervous.

Nicole walked around Candy and looked down at the

boxes Candy seemed almost desperate to hide. "Can I look?"

"Um. Okay." She stood and picked up the box in front of her. "I'll just take this one to the garage since I'm through with it. It doesn't have anything to interest you."

Wrong. What lay on top interested Nicole very much. The framed picture was of John Sanders, Ella's husband—and her father. Ignoring Candy, Nicole reached into the box and lifted out the picture. Beneath it sat a faded blue baseball cap. She lifted that as well, and a gold locket fell to the floor.

Candy dropped the box and covered her face with her hands.

Nicole scooped up the locket. The clasp easily opened to reveal another picture of John Sanders and . . . She lifted her gaze to the older woman, knowing the moment had arrived.

"I didn't want you to find out this way."

"I have to sit down." Nicole sank to the floor, her legs unable to support her. She dipped her hands into the box and came out with a man's large sweatshirt, well-worn, a baseball and a mitt, and a stack of books. Anger started a slow burn in the pit of her stomach. "How did you end up with a box of my father's things when I got nothing? And why didn't you show them to me before?"

"I'm sorry, I should have. I just didn't know how to tell you." Candy looked at her helplessly. "Nicole, your father was the only man I ever loved."

Her anger intensified. "He was married to Ella."

"No, don't misunderstand." Candy's voice was low, resigned. "He loved Ella to distraction. I was just the cute, younger sister."

"Not that much younger," Nicole said, but Candy ignored that. She looked down at her hands, lost in time.

"He never returned the feeling, though he knew. There was a big scene at the end when they left. I'm afraid I professed my love in front of everyone."

"Oh, Candy." Nicole sighed. She could see Candy throwing herself down and begging John not to leave, with her sister and mother watching. "Is that why your mother was so angry?"

"Partly," she replied carefully. "But it's why I was cut off from correspondence and especially the funeral."

"I can't believe it's been you this entire time."

Thunder rumbled, making both women jerk in surprise. Candy smiled nervously. "I'm not very good at this, Nicole. I'm sorry."

The simplicity, the honesty tore at Nicole. Nothing could have melted her the way that quiet statement had. "I'm not good at confrontations either," she admitted. "Though I've become a champ since I came here."

Candy dropped into a chair as if her legs wouldn't support her. "You came to say good-bye?"

"Do you want to say good-bye?"

"No," she whispered with such anguish that Nicole came to sit next to her. Taking Candy's hands wasn't as difficult as she imagined it would be. "Are we ever going to talk about it?"

"About what?" Candy asked uneasily, her hands stiffening in Nicole's.

Nicole made a facetious sound and stood abruptly. "Well, now at least I know where I get it from. You're the master of hedging and avoidance, Candy. I inherited it from the best." She turned away, but not before she saw Candy's color fade at least five shades.

"Have you always known?"

Was that fear in her mother's voice? "No. But you're my mother," Nicole said flatly, whirling back to Candy. "Can't you even say it?" Nothing. "Say it!" Nicole cried, dropping to her knees in front of Candy. "Please, I want to hear you say it." She couldn't even wince at how she pleaded for acknowledgement, there was no pride left.

"Okay," Candy said quietly. "I am your mother."

Nicole jerked to her feet, Candy's admission leaving only an empty feeling in the pit of her stomach. Anticlimactic, she supposed.

"I'm sorry," Candy said, and Nicole's temper frayed.

"You're *sorry*?" Nicole rubbed her hands wearily across her face. "When I think of how happy I was to meet you and the others—well, it's really embarrassing. It must have amused you to fool me so."

"No, no. It wasn't like that at all," Candy said urgently. She stood and paced. "At first I didn't tell you because I was scared. Then later, I didn't know how to without ruining the friendship we'd started. There was no way to tell you, Nicole."

"How about years and years ago? Why didn't you tell me when I was an orphaned infant with nowhere to go? Or how about later, when I was a lost little girl with no one in the world to care? Or even later—I've been in the phone book for *years*. You've got to know I'm dying for information. Why isn't Ella my mother as I thought? Is John Sanders really my father? And—" Nicole's voice caught, and she took a moment before continuing. "Why are you so ashamed of me that you couldn't admit I'm your daughter?"

Candy looked at her, her eyes shimmering. "You don't understand."

The room lit up as a flash of lightning hit, followed

immediately by a strong clap of thunder that had Nicole jumping nervously.

Candy jumped as well. "John was your father," she said into the sudden quiet. "I got pregnant, told Ella it was some deadbeat high-school student so she wouldn't know that her lover had betrayed her with her own sister. She took you simply to protect me and because she wanted a child so badly. You know she could never have her own." She came closer, her eyes locked on Nicole's. "John loved you, Ella loved you, and as far as she was concerned, you were hers."

"Because you didn't want me."

"I wanted you more than you can ever know," she said sadly. "But I was young and foolish. My mother would never have allowed me to keep you, and I was immature enough to allow her to have her way. At least you were with family."

"Until she died. Why didn't you tell me?"

She shrugged helplessly. "So many things, things that now don't make any sense. Ashamed—"

"Don't," Nicole said harshly, flinching at the next bright flash of lightning, bracing for the noisy, disturbing thunder. She moved quickly to the door, unable to tolerate hearing how her mother had been ashamed. "I don't want to hear anymore," she said rashly, lashing out against her own hurt, not thinking of Candy's.

Nicole paused at the door, heartsick. "I wish Ella had been my mother. You betrayed her and my father. No wonder you're ashamed of me, I would be too." She yanked open the door and ran out, though the rain crashed down and the trees whipped each other, creating a noise that terrified Nicole.

"Wait," Candy cried, braced in the doorway. "Don't leave this way. I want to explain."

But Nicole was done with explanations.

"The roads are too slick, Nicole. Please—"

Nicole ignored her as she got into her car. She'd waited forever to talk, and now she was no longer interested. She had to swallow her fear of the storm before she could start her car, and as she drove, she fought the urge to cry.

Alex.

She had to see him.

She drove three quarters of the way on autopilot, refusing to reflect on her actions and trying not to notice the howling winds and driving rain that pelted her car. The rain didn't slow her down, but it was cold, much colder than when she had first left the inn. Night was falling, and her lightweight shorts, blouse, and sandals weren't proper protection against the dropping temperature.

A mile from Alex's she was forced to a complete stop by a long branch lying in the middle of the road. Both lanes were blocked.

Great. She blew the hair from her face and swore.

There wasn't another car in sight. Well, she couldn't go back to Candy's, not after the horrible things she'd said. The rain came down in sheets, dumping gallon buckets at a time. She jerked on her only protection, a sweatshirt. It certainly wouldn't hold out the rain, but it might keep her warm.

She stepped out of the car and directly into a deep puddle. Water oozed past her ankle. With exasperation, she ran to the branch, but it weighed more than she'd guessed.

As if the rain had a sense of humor, it actually came down harder and faster then, and her hair matted itself to her shoulders. The burst of lightning, with the immediate drum of thunder, had her shaking, but she refused to give in. Dragging the branch, she flinched with terror every time the sky lit with jagged lightning, knowing it would be followed by thunder.

When she finished, she leaned against her car, panting, and soaked to the bone. Water ran in small rivers down her face and neck and inside her sweatshirt. With a squishy sound, she sank into her car, shivering a little, but by the time she drove up to Alex's cabin, she couldn't control the violent shudders.

Nicole's heart started to beat ridiculously fast as she ran to his door. Would he turn her away as she had him so many times? She knocked while the wind whipped her face.

He answered the door wearing a weary and distracted expression she'd never seen before, reminding her that he, too, was up to his ears in his own problems. The T-shirt and sweatpants he wore clung to him in a way that made Nicole ache.

"Hi," she said inanely.

He didn't even smile.

FIFTEEN

Alex tossed aside the ledger he held and pulled her in. "Silly fool," he exclaimed, pushing the door closed with his foot, shutting out the storm. "You're drenched."

For Nicole, reality became Alex, warm, dry Alex, not the summer storm that was now muffled by his walls. Shivering as she was, she couldn't speak. He drew down the zipper of her soaking sweatshirt and yanked it off her arms, cursing. "How did you get so wet?"

Her teeth chattered. "B-branch in the road." She tried to relax her painfully tightened muscles so she could talk. "I . . . had to see you, Alex."

His hands stilled and his expression softened. "Come on, let's get you dry." He pulled her through the living room and up the stairs, ignoring her protests that she was dripping everywhere. Finally, she gave up the effort to talk and let him lead her, concentrating on the warm hand that held hers. Halfway up the stairs, she stumbled, then apologized. He merely scooped her up against his body.

"Do you have any idea how dangerous it is to be

driving in a storm like this? Especially in your car?" In the bathroom, he set her down and bent to undo her sandals, swearing again as he touched her icy feet. She held on to his wonderfully strong and solid shoulders as he roughly massaged each one.

"Ouch," she complained as sharp pins stabbed each foot.

"At least you feel them now."

His voice was even, but she could hear something in it. Hurt. She'd done that. She looked down at his dark, bent head and felt a longing so strong, her knees nearly buckled.

She lost her grip on his shoulders as he straightened, so that she had to reach behind her to hold on to the tile for support. He merely shook his head at her, obviously still angry. But she couldn't lift a finger to help him and she couldn't stop trembling if her life depended on it.

"I'll bring you a robe, take off your wet clothes," he said gruffly, turning away.

He glanced back. She hadn't moved and it wrenched another short expletive from him when he realized the extent of her helplessness. Jaw tight, he reached for the buttons on her dripping blouse. After loosening them, he unhooked her bra and, with a deep breath, drew both soggy items down her arms. She still didn't move, couldn't. Wordlessly, he wrapped a towel around her shoulders, murmuring softly to her when she flinched at the sound of thunder. He slid down her soaked shorts and panties next, swallowing audibly when the material clung to her thighs. She stepped out of them and something fell to the floor with a clank.

Alex looked down at the small, smooth pebble he'd sent her so long ago, before she'd ever come back to

Sunrise Valley. "You kept it," he said with obvious pleasure and surprise.

"Yes."

He was still hunkered down before her, his eyes on the pebble as she stood nude before him. "Why?"

"To remind me of you."

He came slowly upright, his heated gaze skimming over her as he rose. He looked into her eyes then, as he slowly encircled her hips with his arms. She sighed and gratefully wrapped her cold limbs around him, inadvertently dropping the towel. She buried her face in his neck. "S-so warm," she mumbled, stuttering with cold. "You're always so w-warm."

She heard him suck in his breath sharply when her bare skin made contact with his shirt. His arms tightened around her, enveloping her in his dry warmth, and passion erupted as forcefully as the next drumroll of thunder.

When he leaned down and captured her mouth with his, she didn't hesitate. It was the best thing that had happened to her all day—in many days. She'd been lacking, needing, craving, and hadn't even realized it. Knowing it now only increased her pleasure. The next hot, deep, all-consuming kiss banished the chill and had her panting for more. She'd been worried he wouldn't want her anymore, but, thankfully, she'd been wrong, very wrong.

But the kiss wasn't enough, not now. With urgent, clumsy fingers, Nicole slid her hands under his T-shirt, feeling bunched muscle, and she closed her eyes to savor the feeling of being near him again.

With a soft oath, he clasped her restless hands in his. "This won't always be enough, Nicole. For either of us."

"For now it is," she said almost desperately. "We'll make it enough. Please, Alex."

Mouth tight, he pulled her from the bathroom into his bedroom, then yanked his own clothes off and gently pushed her down to the bed. She lay back, watching him, knowing she'd never seen a more magnificently made body than his. "You're beautiful, Alex."

He shook his head, his anger abruptly gone, replaced with something much hotter, deeper. "Not like you." He sank beside her, and she pressed herself against him, tilting her hips in the age-old invitation to hurry, to possess. But he refused to do either, chose instead to drive her slowly insane. That mouth of his, that incredibly talented mouth, slowly tormented and enticed hers while his hands slid up and down her stomach and sides with tantalizing languor.

"Put your hands on me," she begged.

"I am." Raining kisses down her neck, along her collarbone, he skimmed fingers over her ribs, and all the while he spoke to her in a low, sexy voice, telling her how he loved her body, what he was going to do to her, and how much she was going to love it. But he still didn't touch her, not where she wanted him to.

"Alex." She grabbed his hand and tried to bring it where she wanted it, but he simply moved it away, letting out a low laugh.

"In a hurry?" he murmured, kissing his way down her neck. "How's this?" he asked, fastening that sexy mouth to an aching, tight nipple, shooting her from impatient arousal to that mindless passion she craved. He worked his mouth over her, driving her up and up, until she could only toss her head back and forth on the pillow, grab handfuls of the sheet. Sliding down over her damp, quivering body, he parted her thighs with his own. Poised above her, he cradled her face in his hands and tilted it to his. She stared into his eyes, so dazed by passion, she couldn't think.

"Nicole," he said in a low, rough voice. "Are you out chasing your demons again, or"—he hesitated, and Nicole saw his uncertainty—"is it me you want?"

Passion and desire clouded his eyes, but there was also a wariness that struck her heart. Reaching out, she held him. "I want *you,*" she whispered, knowing she meant it with all her heart. She lifted her hips against his. "And I'm going to die right here if you don't do something about it."

Lost in the unexpected poignancy of her total surrender, Alex couldn't have controlled or prolonged what happened next if their very lives depended on it.

He drove into her with one thrust. Heaven, he thought as his breath seared his throat, she was absolute heaven. She arched her hips up to meet his, and he almost lost it right there. He'd wanted this for so long, dreamed about it every night, and he could feel her moving desperately beneath him. Her fingers dug into his shoulders, trying to get him in deeper, but he held still, wanting her this way, bucking, clawing, writhing beneath him.

He slipped a hand between their slick bodies to find her. And in one stroke of his thumb, she exploded in his arms, sobbing out his name. Kissing her, he listened to her breathing slow, knowing when she opened those amazing eyes, knowing she wondered why he hadn't moved, yet remained hard as steel within her. She lifted her hips, urging him, and he sucked in his breath, knowing he was close, too close.

"Don't move," he grated. "Please . . . don't move."

She drew back in surprise and met his gaze, running her hands up his taut arms that strained from the effort to control his hot and still-unsatisfied body. "What is it?" she asked in concern. Embarrassment flooded her face. "Did I do something wrong?"

"God, no. It's—we're not using protection," he managed to grind out. The effort not to plunge into her, not to bring them both to the mindless pleasure their bodies craved, was killing him. He pulled out of her, his entire body screaming in protest, and reached for the top drawer of his nightstand, fumbling with the foil packet.

Sitting up, a soft tenderness lit her eyes, and when he'd finished, she pushed him down, spreading a blanket of kisses over his body until he heard himself rasping her name over and over. Slithering her body down over his, her tongue flickered, nibbled, and proceeded to drive him to the very edge.

"Nicole," he gasped as she licked his flat nipple, then clasped her hips to hold her still, knowing she had absolutely no idea what she was doing to him. "Now. God, now."

Smiling, she slid over his body before slowly sinking down on him. "I love you," he whispered roughly.

She swallowed hard and he could see the aching need in her eyes. "I missed you. So much." And he knew that for Nicole, that was a difficult admission. Then she began a slow, deliberate rhythm, rocking her hips in a way that drove him wild. He pulled her down on his chest and gathered her close in his arms, meeting her thrust for thrust. When she cried out and tensed, he kissed her fiercely, his own body shuddering in unison.

Limp, she collapsed on him. Their hearts pounded against each other, their damp limbs entwined. This time, he thought a little dazed, had been even sweeter, hotter, more intense than the last, and infinitely worth the wait.

Nicole's breathing evened out and deepened, and he knew she'd drifted off to sleep. He swept her still-rain-dampened hair from her face and kissed her softly, but she slept the sleep of the exhausted. Having no illusions, he wondered what had driven her to him this time, but didn't have the heart to wake her and ask.

This woman was all he wanted, was all it would take for his life to be perfect. Why couldn't she see that?

He didn't know how long he watched her when the room glowed an eerie blue with the bolt of lightning, a split second before thunder shook the room, vibrating the windows with its force. Nicole jerked out of his arms with a soft cry, covering her ears and clenching her eyes closed.

The terror on her face ripped at him, and he reached for her, his own heart thumping. "Nicole, it's just the storm."

She slumped against him. "The storm?"

He could feel the wild pumping of her heart against his arm. "Just the storm," he told her in a quiet, calm voice, hiding his alarm. "You're okay now, come on, lie back with me." She didn't resist, but clung to him.

"I really hate thunder and lightning," she said, gulping.

"There's nothing to be afraid of now," he said softly, wondering at this seemingly brave woman who crumbled at the sound of thunder.

"I used to hide under my bed until the storm passed," she admitted, burying her face in his neck. "It always seemed to take so long, and I'd be so alone. I hated that."

"You're not alone now, Nicole. And you don't ever have to be again."

Her body relaxed marginally, but she remained silent. He'd thought she'd fallen asleep again until he eased back and saw that her eyes were open.

He could almost hear the complicated wheels of that brain turning. "Are you ever going to tell me what's going on in that gorgeous head of yours, Nicole?" He felt her stiffen again, but he had to know. "What made you come here now . . . tonight?"

"I wanted to see you." She sighed. "I don't know why exactly, except I needed someone and I wanted it to be you."

"Something's happened."

"You could say that." She leaned her head back on his arm and watched his face. "I confronted Candy and it didn't go so well."

Drenched in love and admiration for the woman who'd finally gotten the nerve to face her past, he spoke without thinking. "I didn't get far either," he admitted, squeezing her, wanting to offer comfort. But she surprised him when she sat straight up, clutching the sheet to her, staring at him with wild eyes. "You talked to her about me. You never said anything."

She tried to leap from the bed, but Alex lunged for her and held her fast. "Wait!"

"Did you two have a good laugh, Alex?" she cried, struggling fiercely. "Poor Nicole," she said, choking. "Her mother's really her aunt and her aunt's really her mother, only she's too ashamed to admit it!"

"That's not how it is," he ground out, clenching his teeth when her knee rammed hard into his thigh. "Dammit, stop it!" He wrapped his arms around her and threw a leg over hers. When the fight went out of her, he gentled his hold and lowered his voice. "It wasn't like that. I wanted her to tell you."

"But she didn't," Nicole whispered, staring at him with reproach. "I had to figure it out by stealing files."

He hated the way she looked at him, as if there wasn't a person in the world she could trust. "I tried to push things along by insisting you talk to her, but when I couldn't get you to do that, I went to Candy. I pressured her to tell you. If she didn't, I would have."

She stared at him. "You . . . did that for me?"

He nodded, touching her face. "Yeah. I wanted you to know. You deserved to know. Did she tell you why she'd hidden it?" He frowned when she didn't answer. "Don't tell me you didn't talk to her about it."

"I told you, it didn't go so well."

He knew that defensive tone. "Nicole, you ran out on her, didn't you?"

"She's ashamed of me. What other reason is there for not telling me?"

"I don't know. You should have asked her."

"It doesn't matter." She shrugged, pulling away. "Summer's almost over anyway."

He stared at her, reading what he didn't want to know in her stubborn refusal to meet his eyes, in the hard set line of her jaw, in the stiff way she held her body. "You're leaving," he said flatly. "You're going back to San Francisco as if none of this ever happened."

"My job starts up again soon," she reminded him in a calm voice that completely defied her heart's frantic beat against his.

"You could stay here."

"I could," she said lightly. "But I've grown fond of eating." She covered herself with the sheet. "I need the money, Alex."

"So I'll pay you more for your work at the inn. Or get a teaching job here. Or come work at the resort. Hell, I don't care if you do nothing, just stay." He looked at the closed expression on her face. "This is another avoidance tactic."

"Really?" She looked amused, damn her. "What am I avoiding?"

He sat up, too angry to realize he was completely naked. "Us."

"Coming here tonight wasn't a good idea," she said, sighing. "It just complicated things for you."

That angered him, but watching her retreat emotionally before his very eyes terrified him more. "You've built a wall around you, and you won't let anyone in."

"It's easier that way."

He shook his head, angry at her and angry at himself for letting her do it—until now. "You're cheating yourself and everyone who cares about you."

"I give everything I have," she said defensively, backing up a step as he stood. "What could I possibly be cheating myself and others of?"

"Love."

She paled, and he knew his words had hit the mark. Fear swam in her eyes, and he nearly staggered as he realized what was the matter.

She was afraid of love.

Her hesitancy, her family's deceptions, it was all an excuse. Anger drained as compassion welled up within him. He understood that this incredibly enduring woman before him didn't know how to give love because she'd never been shown love.

"I love you," he said with quiet conviction.

She made a disbelieving noise, but the pulse at the

base of her neck went wild. He could almost taste her fear.

"I do. I'd tell you that every day for the rest of your life if you'd let me."

Nicole's mouth dropped open, and she backed away from him.

"I can see that flatters the hell out of you," he muttered, following her. He reached for her, and she felt trapped against his broad shoulders, the solid wall of muscle that was his chest and . . . the rest of his naked body.

He leaned down until their lips nearly touched. "I love you," he repeated in a deep, velvety voice.

He couldn't have any idea how those words made her feel. "Don't say that," she whispered.

"What are you afraid of? Me loving you or the fact that you love me back?"

Anger surged through her veins, traveling hot and quick like fire, chasing away the weakness she'd felt at his words, his tone, his closeness. Anger gave her strength. "How can you be so sure I love you?"

"Don't you?" His mouth came down on hers in a scorching kiss that was rough and hot. She could have managed to resist that if she tried hard enough, but he abruptly gentled himself, and there was no protection against the onslaught of tenderness, compassion, and understanding he put into that kiss. Brushing his parted lips over hers in a light, teasing touch, he used his hands to caress her face. When he finally pulled back, he stared into her eyes, and she felt as though her soul had been stripped naked.

"Admit it, Nicole," he whispered in a soft, gruff voice. "You love me."

When he looked at her that way, she couldn't think.

She opened her mouth to tell him so, but his mouth took hers again. He held the back of her head, while his other arm drifted down to snuggle her hips tight against his. And she completely lost herself in the swirling sensations. Pressed to his naked body from head to toe, she could think of nothing but him. Against his chest, her fists flattened, her hands slid up and around his neck, and she found herself kissing him back with all she had, her confusion and desperation set aside.

A powerful thunderclap split the room, and with it, sanity returned. Pulling back, panting, she covered her wet mouth.

He'd been trying to seduce her into saying she loved him.

"That wasn't fair! You can't make me say it."

"I wasn't trying to trick you, Nicole," he said solemnly, his eyes dark with desire, his body fully aroused.

Nicole had never been so aware of her own nudity, or of his. She bent down, picked up his discarded shirt, and slipped into it, trying to swallow her panic. Once she had the shirt buttoned, she felt in a better position to argue. "I've never said those words before," she admitted, her voice hard with anger and hurt. "You can't bully me into it."

"I would never bully you into anything." He yanked on his pants, but didn't fasten them. He was much more interested in pacing the room.

"I can't stay, Alex."

"Tell me one good reason," he challenged. "And the job doesn't count."

"You make it sound so easy," she cried, leaning against the bed. She needed the support because the anger, hurt, and love on his face was too much for her to bear. "It isn't. I have a life hundreds of miles from here."

"No," he agreed readily. "It isn't easy. I just want it more than you do, I guess."

His bitter expression made her want to cry.

"What is it *you* want, Nicole?" he asked wearily.

She glanced around at his warm, beautiful surroundings. "I just want to know where my home is. I want to be with people who know who I am, and with people who love me for that."

His voice vibrated with deep emotion. "I know where there's a home with someone in it who loves you very much."

Her heart stopped. "Alex—"

He touched a hand to her lips to stop her protest. "Forget it." He gathered up her wet clothes, looking discouraged and disappointed. "I'll go dry these."

The finality on his face scared her. She followed him down the stairs. "Why does it have to be this way? We can still see each other after I'm gone. It's only a couple of hours away."

He whirled around on the stairs so fast, she plowed into him. The look he shot her was born of pure frustration. "So we'll get together for a day every couple of weeks when one of us manages to get off?" He shook his head. "That would work for a while, maybe. But I want more, Nicole. I want to see you, talk to you, hold you . . . love you. I want a family—*with you.* Anything less than that won't satisfy me for long, and it sure as hell shouldn't work for you either."

He turned and went down the stairs, halting in front of the large sliding-glass door in the living room. She came up beside him, aching at the hurt on his face. "Why can't we simply enjoy what we have for now?"

"Nicole, you grew up that way, bounced from home to home. You hated it. How can you still want to live like that?" Tossing the clothes down into a heap on the floor, he leaned a hand on the wood frame of the slider and sighed.

She dropped into a chair. After a minute he came toward her, stopping when their toes touched. Her knees bumped against his lower legs. He wound his fingers into her hair and turned her face up.

"By your own admission you want a real home, someone close to your heart who loves you." His thumbs rubbed soothing circles on her cheeks and neck. "You've got that, Nicole. I love you with all my heart."

Her eyes stung, but she blinked back the urge to cry. Crouching before her, he whispered, "You still can't trust, can you? Still running, always afraid to let anyone too close because you'll lose them eventually. Even if you have to push them away."

"You'll be better off without me," she said.

"No. I need you."

"You don't." She'd never met a more confident, self-reliant man in her life. He looked at her expectantly and it scared her. "You want something from me that I'm not capable of giving."

He shook his head. "You've got yourself convinced you're not worthy of love, that no one could ever love you. You're wrong, Nicole, I promise you. You can do this."

She surged to her feet and walked to the window, resting her forehead against the cool glass. The view caught her breath. The spectacular valley lay below, and the moon cast its soft, white glow over the peaks and valleys of the mountains. Sunrise Valley in all its splendor. It felt like . . . home.

"Have I ever lied to you, Nicole?"

He stood behind her. She shook her head, still staring out the window. "No."

"I never will. I'm a man of my word," he said with quiet dignity that had Nicole's heart lurching. "I say only what I mean."

She believed that. But she still couldn't give him what he wanted.

SIXTEEN

Nicole got back to the inn very late, but Susan was waiting for her.

"I thought you'd left," Susan said carefully as they sat together at the table in the kitchen. "I thought you'd given up and left."

Nicole's hands stilled on the sugar she added to her tea. "You've talked to Candy, then."

"Yes," Susan admitted. "I didn't know about her being your mother, Nicole." She hesitated. "I'm so sorry."

"It's okay."

"No, it's not. Not if you're going to leave."

"I'm not leaving because of that." Wasn't she? "I have work. My home is in the city."

"What about us? Will you miss us?"

Nicole pushed her tea away. "Of course," she said, thinking of Alex. Was he right? Would casual visits kill what they had?

"You'll leave us with sorrow, Nicole. Did you know that you've helped me change? That because of you, I was able to let go of a lifetime of bitterness?"

Nicole gave her a long look. "I doubt that."

"It's true," Susan insisted, then blushed faintly. "I never thought I'd actually admit this, but I'm a big part of the reason Alex had so much trouble with his day-care center." She looked down at her hands. "I caused him a lot of trouble, and probably a lot of money, simply because I wanted to hurt him."

"Oh, Susan." Nicole sighed and took her hand. "You didn't."

"I did. I managed nearly to put a halt to that expansion he wants so badly, simply because I was bitter. I fixed it," she said quickly, lifting her head. "And I'm really sorry for it, but I can't take it back. I can only make it better. And without you, I don't know if I would have ever been able to change."

"How in the world did I help you?"

Susan smiled. "You gave me something no one else did. Yourself."

Nicole stared at her, stunned.

"You came here because I asked you to. You helped me simply because I needed it. Even when I didn't deserve it, you believed in me. You were my friend."

Nicole cleared her throat past the lump that stuck there.

"You'll hurt Alex if you leave."

"He didn't tell you that." Nicole felt certain.

"The grapevine around here is wonderfully accurate." Susan shrugged. "I should know. I used to run it."

Nicole didn't fall asleep until dawn, and then it was a fitful, restless sleep filled with nightmares.

In her dreams she drove back to the city. Her apartment sat just as she'd left it, stark and clean. No mail waiting. No messages on her machine. No one cared, no one loved her. No one ever would, because she wouldn't let them.

But she was wrong, a little voice cried. Her family did love her. Alex loved her. She hopped back into her car and raced back to Sunrise Valley. But something was wrong, very wrong.

The Wilson House looked deserted. The halls were eerily silent. Susan couldn't be found. Alarmed, Nicole drove to Candy's house, jumped out of her car, and pounded on the door. No one answered her desperate knock.

Panicked now, she drove to Ted's house. Same thing. No one answered. Swallowing her fear, she tried the hospital.

No Brad.

She hurried to Alex's cabin, but it was empty. So was the resort and Alex's office. She'd pushed them all away, denied their love.

She had no one.

Nicole sat straight up in bed at the inn, panting with fear and panic. She grasped at the antique quilt on the bed, nearly crying in relief at the realization it had all been a dream and she was still at Sunrise Valley.

But she was still alone. She had a vision of herself ten, twenty, even thirty years from now, still alone in her bed, still wishing for family around her.

Still pushing people away.

She'd been a complete fool, she told herself, whipping the covers off. A complete fool, and it'd be her own fault if it was too late to fix it.

She wanted Alex.

She could never get him out of her mind, or her heart, and she'd been ridiculous to think she could. She'd been running so hard and so fast from the truth, she didn't even recognize it. She'd managed to evade getting answers about her family until it was time for her to leave the small town, because those answers meant she might have a permanent relationship with her family. Or with Alex.

He'd offered her his heart on a golden platter, and she'd pushed it away, convinced she didn't need it. *She did.* She'd walked away from the love of a lifetime.

She couldn't let her dream become a reality.

She dressed in an insane rush. By the time she got downstairs, she was shaking with the hurry to prove her dream wouldn't—couldn't—be true.

Susan was nowhere to be found.

It's a coincidence, Nicole assured herself, running to her car. A sick coincidence that she couldn't find her cousin after her nightmare. She drove like a maniac to Alex's cabin.

No answer. Oh, God.

Her breath caught in her throat as she ran down the path to the resort. Her nightmare was coming true. She'd waited too long. Desperation clutched her so, she could hardly breathe. She ran to the lodge, her vision blurry with tears. Was she still dreaming? She had to be.

When she heard the distant hum of an electric tool, her heart soared with hope. Yanking open the heavy double doors of the lodge, she blinked against the dim light, and was rewarded when the hum grew louder. But the building was huge, and she couldn't tell from which direction the noise came.

"Hello?" she called out, her voice echoing. "Hello!" She ran to the cafeteria, but in the room filled with steel counters and appliances, she couldn't get her bearings.

On the second floor, the humming grew louder. Then stopped abruptly. She walked around, up and down the various stairwells, but all she could hear was her own footsteps.

Her panic returned, a hundred times worse than before. Suddenly weak, she plopped down on a step in the dim stairway. Whoever had been working had obviously left.

Why had she ever wanted to be alone?

And why had she ever thought she could live without Alex? His sexy smile, his sense of humor, his quiet decisiveness did something to her she couldn't explain. And his incredible laugh that never failed to turn her heart on its side—the very same organ that was now being ripped to pieces by her own stupidity.

Then she heard a light footstep above her and looked up as Alex's long legs came into view. He wore that same leather jacket she loved, the one that showed off his broad, lean frame so well. He looked good, she thought, better than good, but there wasn't that quiet decisiveness or his smile about him now.

Nicole waited, hoping he'd say something. Anything.

"Hello, Nicole," he said finally.

She didn't plan it, but she couldn't have stopped the sudden flow of tears if she wanted to. They poured steadily and unchecked down her cheeks until she covered her face with both hands, overcome by embarrassment and her own emotions. But still, she couldn't stop.

With a sigh, he folded himself down next to her. Without a word, he reached for her, pulling her into his arms with surprising warmth and compassion.

"Things that bad?" he asked, resting his chin on her head.

"Worse." His familiar scent, the closeness of him, and the rightness of the feel of him only reinforced her earlier thoughts. Gulping, hiccuping, she told him of her dream. "I was all alone, and so scared because I couldn't find anyone."

"I was your last choice?"

Leaning back to deny that, to tell him he was her first and only choice, she saw the humor sparkling in his eyes, mixed in with something else too. Relief.

She pressed closer to him. "I don't want to be without you, Alex. I don't know what I was thinking."

He squeezed her tighter, and she felt love fill her empty heart. Joy surged through her veins. "I can't keep pushing people away because I'm scared," she said shakily.

"Right," he agreed, plunging his hands in her hair and kissing her.

"But it's terrifying," she said against his mouth.

He lifted his head a fraction, stared into her eyes. "I know. But believe me, it's worth it."

Feeling incredibly unburdened, she smiled at him. He kissed her then, long and with a complete thoroughness that robbed her of all conscious thought.

"You want to be with me?" he questioned, looking at her with that familiar heated gaze.

The kiss had left her giddy and dizzy. "Always."

"Will you marry me, then?"

She felt his sudden nervous tension in the way his arms banded like steel around her. She laughed, and it felt good. "Yes."

His arms tightened. "And live with me?"

"I've always wanted the small-town life."

He made a face. "I don't care where we live, Nicole. I just want to be with you."

She couldn't imagine him anywhere but in Sunrise Valley, but knowing he'd give it up for her had her eyes filling again. "I want to live here." She could see her admission had left him momentarily dazzled, but he didn't appear totally convinced.

"What if you can't teach here?" he asked. "You love to teach."

"I love you more."

His breath caught and he squeezed her so tight, she thought he might crack a rib. Then he held her face so she could see his eyes, shimmering brightly with his own emotion. "I love you," he whispered fiercely, then gave her another smoldering kiss to prove it.

SEVENTEEN

"You're thinking about Candy," Alex guessed. He let go of Nicole's hand as they started up the path from the lodge to his cabin and put his arm around her to pull her closer. He didn't think he could ever have her close enough.

She looked at him funny. "That might get annoying."

"What?"

"The way you read my mind. How am I supposed to stay mad at you if I can't ever have a private thought? Yes, I'm thinking of Candy. *My mother.*"

He stopped, turned her to him. Above them, in the morning air, the birds chattered noisily. The sun warmed them. "First of all, get mad at me all you want. Just don't keep it to yourself. And if you're thinking of Candy, why don't we go talk to her? I bet that would make her day."

"I can't," she said, her voice shaking. "Tell me again, Alex."

He smiled. "I love you." He squeezed her tight at the look of wonder on her face.

"I'll never get tired of hearing that." She sighed. "I love you too."

Her love humbled him, but she was changing the subject. "Why can't you go talk to Candy? You want to."

"Yes, I want to." She chewed her lip and looked at him with those deep amber eyes in a way that had him momentarily distracted. "I wasn't very nice to her the last time we spoke."

"So apologize." He kissed her gently, hoping to banish the worry from her eyes. What he got was a look of such pure love, it staggered him.

"I'm afraid she'll tell me to get lost. It's pretty much what I told her to do." She looked away, and Alex knew she fully expected him to scorn her.

He squeezed her hands until she looked at him, then brought her fingers to his lips. "I bet she doesn't." He pulled her back down the small incline to the open clearing by the lodge, then reached into his pocket. "Here," he said, holding up a quarter and gesturing to the pay phone against the wall of the wooden lodge. "Call her and see."

She took the quarter, flipped it over in her hand. She smiled at him nervously and walked to the phone.

She dialed slowly, and he watched her carefully, his heart beating fast in excitement for her. He knew how important this moment was, for all of them. It had to work out, he thought. Nicole had to learn to be comfortable with her past.

Then he realized she was off the phone and staring at him. Her eyes shone brightly.

"What did she say?" he demanded.

"Brad woke up. They've been at the hospital all

morning. That's why Susan wasn't in the inn when I went downstairs. She'd left me a note, I must have missed it." Her voice shook with emotion. "And Candy said—" Her voice broke with a sob.

"What?" he pushed, hugging her. "She said what?"

Her smile was tremulous and brilliant. "She said to hurry home."

THE EDITORS' CORNER

People often ask how we can keep track of all the LOVESWEPTs, the authors and their stories, and good grief, all the characters! It's actually pretty easy. We're fortunate to have some of the most talented authors writing for us, telling beautiful stories about memorable and endearing characters. To lose track of them would be like losing track of what's going on in the lives of our closest friends! The August LOVESWEPT lineup is no exception to the rule. We hope you enjoy these stories as much as we did!

First up is Loveswept favorite Laura Taylor, who leaves us all breathless with **ANTICIPATION,** LOVESWEPT #846. Viva Conrad fled Kentucky without warning, leaving behind a life she adored and silencing her dreams in a gamble to keep the people she loved safe. Spencer Hammond will stop at nothing to discover the truth of her desertion and her involvement in his stepbrother's death. Brought together by the wishes of a dead man and a racehorse guaranteed to win it all, Viva and Spencer must learn to tolerate each other for the good of their investment. As their individual agendas collide, the two must also deal with the unexpected attraction that flares to life between them, amid secrets that threaten to destroy what they long to build together. Suspense rivals sensuality in Laura Taylor's riveting saga of dangerous secrets and shadowy seductions.

Next on the docket, Peggy Webb returns with an exciting romp through the southern part of heaven with a man who can only be referred to as Tarzan on a Harley. After having headed for the hills to forget a thoughtless scoundrel, B. J. Corban is now stuck with the job of **BRINGING UP BAXTER**, LOVESWEPT #847. Baxter, you see, is this cute little puppy who's trying to steal everyone's heart (and the limelight as well). However, when B. J. gets a look at the muscular legs encased in the tight leather pants of Crash Beauregard, she scents danger and irresistible possibilities. Prim lawyer that she is, B. J. tries to resist the devilish charms of the sexy rebel. Peggy teases and tempts with delicious wit and delectable humor as she reveals just what happens when a big-city lawyer and a judge from the sticks tangle over a case of true love.

Detective Aaron Stone desperately needs a break in the murder investigation of notorious drug dealer Owen Blake in **BLACK VELVET**, LOVESWEPT #848 by Kristen Robinette. So when a phone call comes through for the deceased dealer, Aaron jumps on this new lead. On a lark, Katherine Jackson tries to contact the man of her dreams, just to see if he really exists. When they meet, the attraction sizzles and Aaron must now decide whether this woman with the face of an angel bears the heart of a killer. Katherine's dreams begin to reveal more secrets, this time involving Aaron. These secrets evoke more emotions than Aaron can bear and it's up to Katherine to give him new hope where none had seemed possible. Kristen Robinette's story is woven of equal parts mesmerizing mystery and heartbreaking emotion and is guaranteed to touch your heart, as a man's heart is slowly healed by the love of his life.

Please welcome newcomer Kathy DiSanto, who gives us a story about a man struggling to decide if women want him **FOR LOVE OR MONEY,** LOVESWEPT #849. Acting on a dare has never worked out well for teacher Jennifer Casey. But when she's *triple-dog* dared to write a letter to millionaire Brent Maddox, her pride leaves her no choice. When he shows up at her doorstep with a dare of his own, Jen must spend a week with Brent in his "natural habitat" to see how the other half lives. Hobnobbing with the rich and famous has taught Jen that their lives are vastly different from hers, but can Brent teach her otherwise? As their tempers collide and their hearts unite, Jen and Brent must build a bridge between their two worlds. Kathy's romantic tale of two unlikely lovers is fast-paced and funny—and one you'll never forget!

By now you guys must have seen the new LOVESWEPT look. We hope you are as pleased with it as we are. Please let us know what you think by writing to us in care of Joy Abella, or even visiting our BDD Online web site (http://www.bdd.com/romance)!

Happy reading!

With warmest regards,

Shauna Summers Joy Abella

Shauna Summers	Joy Abella
Editor	Administrative Editor

P.S. Look for these Bantam women's fiction titles coming in August. From Deborah Smith, one of the freshest voices in romantic fiction, comes **A PLACE TO CALL HOME**, an extraordinary love story begun in childhood friendship and rekindled after twenty years of separation. Bestselling author Jane Feather is back with **THE SILVER ROSE**, the second book in her "Charm Bracelet Trilogy," a tale of two noble families, the legacy of an adulterous passion, and the feud that threatens to spill more blood . . . or bind two hearts against all odds.

From the bestselling author of *Breath of Magic* and *Shadows and Lace* comes a beguiling new time-travel love story in the hilarious, magical voice that has made **Teresa Medeiros** one of the nation's most beloved romance writers.

TOUCH OF ENCHANTMENT

Heiress Tabitha Lennox considered her paranormal talents a curse, so she dedicated her life to the cold, rational world of science. Until the day she examined the mysterious amulet her mother left her and found herself catapulted seven centuries into the past—directly into the path of a chain-mailed warrior. . . . Sir Colin of Ravenshaw had returned from the Crusades to find his enemy poised to overrun the land. The last thing he expected was to narrowly avoid trampling a damsel with odd garb and even odder manners. But it is her strange talent that will create trouble beyond Colin's wildest imaginings. For everyone knows that a witch must be burned—and Colin's heart is already aflame. . . .

He thought the creature was female, but he couldn't be sure. Any hint of its sex was buried beneath a shapeless tunic and a pair of loose leggings. It blinked up at him, its gray eyes startlingly large in its pallid face.

"Who the hell are you?" he growled. "Did that murdering bastard send you to ambush me?"

It lifted its cupped hands a few inches off the ground. "Do I look like someone sent to ambush you?"

The thing had a point. It wore no armor and carried no weapon that he could see, unless you counted those beseeching gray eyes. Definitely female, he decided with a grunt of mingled relief and pain. He might have been too long without a woman, but he'd yet to be swayed by any of the pretty young lads a few of his more jaded comrades favored.

"Have you no answer for? Who the hell are you?"

To his surprise, the surly demand ignited a spark of spirit in the wench's eyes. "Wait just a minute! Maybe the question should be, Who the hell are *you*?" Her eyes narrowed in a suspicious glare. "Don't I know you?" She began to mutter beneath her breath as she studied his face, making him wonder if he hadn't snared a lunatic. "Trim the hair. Give him a shave and a bath. Spritz him with Brut and slip him into an off-the-rack suit. Aha!" she crowed. "You're George, aren't you? George . . . George . . . ?" She snapped her fingers. "George Ruggles from Accounting!" She slanted him a glance that was almost coy. "Fess up now, Georgie boy. Did Daddy offer you a raise to play knight in shining armor to my damsel in distress?"

His jaw went slack with shock as she swatted his sword aside and scrambled to her feet, brushing the grass from her shapely rump with both hands. "You can confide in me, you know. I promise it won't affect your Yearly Performance Evaluation."

She was taller than he had expected, taller than any woman of his acquaintance. But far more disconcerting than her height was her brash attitude. Since he'd been old enough to wield a sword, he'd never met anyone, man or woman, who wasn't afraid of him.

The sun was beating down on his head like an anvil. He clenched his teeth against a fresh wave of pain. "You may call me George if it pleases you, my lady, but 'tis *not* my name."

She paced around him, making the horse prance and shy away from her. "Should I call you Prince then? Or will Mr. Charming do? And what would you like to call me? Guenevere perhaps?" She touched a hand to her rumpled hair and batted her sandy eyelashes at him. "Or would you prefer Rapunzel?"

His ears burned beneath her incomprehensible taunts. He could think of several names he'd like to call her, none of them flattering. A small black cat appeared out of nowhere to scamper at her heels, forcing him to rein his stallion in tighter or risk trampling them both. Each nervous shuffle of the horse's hooves jarred his aching bones.

She eyed his cracked leather gauntlets and tarnished chain mail with blatant derision. "So where's your shining armor, Lancelot? Is it back at the condo being polished or did you send it out to the dry cleaners?"

She paced behind him again. All the better to slide a blade between his ribs, he thought dourly. Resisting the urge to clutch his shoulder, he wheeled the horse around to face her. The simple motion made his ears ring and his head spin.

"Cease your infernal pacing, woman!" he bellowed. "Or I'll—" He hesitated, at a loss to come up with a threat vile enough to stifle this chattering harpy.

She flinched, but the cowed look in her eyes was quickly replaced by defiance. "Or you'll what?" she demanded, resting her hands on her hips. "Carry me off to your castle and ravish me? Chop my saucy little head off?" She shook her head in disgust. "I can't believe Mama thought I'd fall for this chauvinistic crap. Why didn't she just hire a mugger to knock me over the head and steal my purse?"

She marched away from him. Ignoring the warning throb of his muscles, he drove the horse into her path. Before she could change course again, he hefted his sword and nudged aside the fabric of her tunic, bringing the blade's tip to bear against the swell of her left breast. Her eyes widened and she took several hasty steps backward. He urged the stallion forward, pinioning her against the trunk of a slender oak. As her gaze met his, he would have almost sworn he could feel her heart thundering beneath the blade's dangerous caress.

A mixture of fear and doubt flickered through her eyes. "This isn't funny anymore, Mr. Ruggles," she said softly. "I hope you've kept your résumé current, because after I tell my father about this little incident, you'll probably be needing it."

She reached for his blade with a trembling hand, stirring reluctant admiration in him. But when she jerked her hand back, her fingertips were smeared with blood.

At first he feared he had pricked her in his clumsiness. An old shame quickened in his gut, no less keen for its familiarity. He'd striven not to harm any woman since he'd sworn off breaking hearts.

She did not yelp in distress or melt into a swoon. She simply stared at her hand as if seeing it for the first time. "Doesn't feel like ketchup," she muttered, her words even more inexplicable than her actions. She sniffed at her fingers. "Or smell like cherry cough syrup."

As her bewildered gaze met his and the ringing in his ears deepened to an inescapable roaring, he realized what she had already discovered. 'Twas not her blood staining her breast, but his own.

He slumped over the horse's neck, clutching at the coarse mane. He could feel his powerful legs weakening, betrayed by the weight of the chain mail that was supposed to protect him. Sweat trickled into his eyes, its relentless sting blinding him.

"Go," he gritted out. "Leave me be."

At first he thought she would obey. He heard her skitter sideways, then hesitate, poised on the brink of flight.

Swaying in the saddle, he pried open his eyes to cast her a beseeching glance. Sir Colin of Ravenshaw had never fallen before anyone, especially not a woman.

And in the end he didn't fall before this one either.

He fell on her.

Sometimes the only thing standing in the way of true love is true friendship. . . .

REMEMBER THE TIME

by Annette Reynolds

An emotional, powerful story that celebrates all the joys, fears, and passions of true love.

They were the best of friends since high school, an inseparable threesome: Kate Moran, Paul Armstrong, and Mike Fitzgerald. But it was Paul who won Kate's heart and married her, leaving Mike to love Kate from afar. Then, in a tragic accident, Paul died, and for Kate, it was as if she had lost her life, too. Now, after nearly three years of watching Kate mourn, of seeing the girl who loved life become a woman who suffers through it, Mike knows he can't hold back any longer. The time has come to tell her how he feels. And all he can hope is that Kate recognizes what he's known all along: that they've always been perfect for each other. But there are secrets that can shake even the strongest bonds of love and friendship . . . and betrayals that can tear two lovers apart.